THE BUTTERFLY MAN

Retta Christian

Jan-Carol
Publishing, Inc
"every story needs a book"

The Butterfly Man
Retta Christian
Published November 2024
Little Creek Books
Imprint of Jan-Carol Publishing, Inc.
All rights reserved
Copyright © 2024 Retta Christian

ISBN: 978-1-962561-51-8
Library of Congress Control Number: 2024947946

You may contact the publisher:
Jan-Carol Publishing, Inc.
PO Box 701
Johnson City, TN 37605
publisher@jancarolpublishing.com
www.jancarolpublishing.com

To Rick,

Thank you for your support throughout this journey.
Your help was invaluable, your advice spot on,
and your example impeccable.
Love you more.

Author's Note

Heroes don't always come equipped with capes and flamboyant gestures. Heroes are people in your circle who take your hand and pull you through, pull you up, sometimes push you over when necessary, and set you back on track. I wanted to highlight the day-to-day, the unrecognized who are taken for granted but who are why we thrive and carry on when the road becomes rocky. These special ones give us hope and strength to continue the game. A smile, a nod, and an encouraging word has made all the difference in my life. Sometimes we need direction. A life-changing hug from someone with good intentions can save a life eventually. A hero without a sign. So, if you need a hero, you may not have to look too far. They could be right in front of you.

Part One

Rick

Only two sounds could be heard in the quiet country cemetery under the cloudless blue sky—the insistent sound of cicadas and the soft voice of a lone mourner.

Rick Morgan stood before his wife's grave under the old and weathered oak tree, feeling awkward and holding onto the now withered white roses he had purchased for her that morning. They had always been her favorite. He had been updating Lisa on their boys.

Lisa, his wife of over thirty years, had died six months ago today. A broken heart had kept him away. Denial. Standing there looking at the date had made it real for him and seeing her name and the butterfly that their oldest son, John, had added to her marker. Rick bent over, placed the flowers on the grave, touched his index finger and middle finger to his lips, then touched her chiseled name with the same fingers.

"I love you, babe," came out in a hoarse whisper. Rick missed his wife.

Images of the past flooded his memory, freezing him to the spot for a moment. He turned and walked through the lines of markers back to his black 2000 Dodge Ram. He had bought it over twenty years ago. It wasn't worth much, but it still ran good enough for a work vehicle. It held sentimental value for him mostly.

He climbed in the truck with intentions of heading to his Kenworth and leaving for Waddy, Kentucky. He hadn't taken one day off since Lisa died. Hadn't made it home. Still couldn't step back into the house they had shared for over 30 years. The Pilot still provided showers and food when he needed it. He thought maybe it was time he came to see Lisa at the graveside. He didn't know what to expect. He kept his feelings to himself mostly; this was too much for him right now, so like always, he called the kids. His daily check-in. He didn't inform them that he had come home. The call gave them comfort. He sounded okay; that's all that mattered.

* * *

Rick drifted into the parking lot where he kept his truck, climbed down, and slipped a $50.00 check into the slot provided beside the office door to pay for truck parking for the month, as well as a small storage building that he kept for his tools and truck parts. It was time to head out again. He called dispatch to get his trailer number, jotted down some numbers in his logbook after his pre-trip inspection was done, and headed out.

* * *

The sound of the engine brought some pleasure to Rick's troubled mind. He liked having a purpose. Being in control of something. He kept putting one foot in front of the other. Doing the job. Work was all he knew. He enjoyed it. Now, he needed it. The job was his raft in an ocean of chaos and pain.

Something solid to hold onto for right now.

* * *

350 miles. All alone with his thoughts, then bedtime, all alone with his dreams. Neither appealed to him right now. Both brought measured loneliness and pain and added weight to the ache that would never go away.

Rick turned on the radio. Fox News was still talking about the effects of Covid-19. He turned the volume down. Traffic jam up ahead. He rolled down the window to get some fresh air and to listen to the sounds of traffic.

A pretty Monarch butterfly flew in the window and landed on his gear shifter. Wings batting to and fro.

Lisa had loved butterflies. She had collected items with butterflies on them. Rick had enjoyed finding trinkets with butterflies on them to bring home to her. If she had been alive, he would have called home and said something like, "Guess what, Lisa? A friend of yours is sitting in the truck with me."

She would have named it. She had named everything. Their plants, cars, trucks, jewelry, our willow tree. She had named our tree Willow after one of her favorite characters.

"Willow, that's what I'll name you," Rick said to the butterfly. Rick figured she'd fly out, but even after the truck started moving again, Willow stayed put. Rick kept the window cracked enough for her to fly back out of the passenger side window when she wanted to.

Two hours into the trip, Rick pulled into a fuel stop, rolled the window down a little more, but not enough to welcome anyone with bad intentions. No point in making it easy. If a man wanted something, he was going to have to work for it. That included stealing.

He figured Willow would be gone when he got back. He left the truck running and pocketed his keys after topping off with 175 gallons of fuel. He walked into the truck stop to pay for his fuel and to pick up a few necessities, fill up his thermos with coffee, and go to the bathroom.

* * *

Rick was hungry. He hadn't eaten anything all day. Twelve diet Pepsis and a thermos of coffee was his usual throughout the day. A cheeseburger appealed to him. He stopped at the counter and ordered one. No onions, no fries, and a cup of ice to add to his Yeti when he got back in the truck. He always kept a case of diet Pepsi in the back of the truck. Lisa had always made sure he was stocked up. That was his job now.

He said thank you to Grace, the cashier, and asked about her three kids. Used some of his fuel points to purchase three candy bars to send home to them. Grace had been working at the Pilot for ten years that Rick knew of. She was in her forties now, raising three kids on her own. Always cheerful and kind.

* * *

As he got back in the truck, he started thinking about his boys—Steve, a workaholic like his dad; John, the baby finishing up his law degree; and Scott, raising a kid of his own. Good kids. He was a proud father.

He got in the seat and got comfortable. He poured the ice into his Yeti, added his Pepsi to the ice, unwrapped the burger and prepared to eat, pulling back the paper for his first bite. It smelled so good.

Then out of nowhere, the butterfly flew into his line of vision and startled him. His burger dropped to the floor. He had forgotten about Willow and was very surprised that she was still here.

"Well, Willow, I guess you're here to keep my cholesterol down," Rick said with a smile.

Grace

Grace Ferguson had known Rick Morgan since they were in kindergarten together. He was a good man.

He had helped her out after Dan, her sorry excuse for a husband, had left her alone with three young kids. Even when he was having a hard time himself, Rick would use his fuel points to buy snacks for her kids and send them home with her. The kids still talk about that, and Rick still sends them snacks. Money for Christmas and birthdays, too.

He always spoke well of Lisa. Grace had gotten to know her over the years by talking to Rick and through her nosey coworker, Anne. Anne knew Lisa from when they used to be neighbors. Small world.

Anne had said to Grace one day, "Never knew a woman to love a man like that, but then, Rick is easy to love from what I hear. He has been a good husband. Making him happy just made her happy. I heard her say it a hundred times. Good momma to those three kids, too. You'd never know they weren't hers, never heard either one of them say that they were adopted. I just knew they didn't have any, then they had three."

Lisa had worked in the foster system. She couldn't have kids and wanted to work with kids that needed her. She quit her job in Social Services and went to work for AMI Kids, a foster care group. She fell in love with three little boys, brought them home, and never looked back. It was what she was born to do. Those boys blossomed under her care and nurturing spirit for sure. Rick was thrilled. He loved being a father to those three boys. Took right to it.

Grace had a crush on Rick. Anne did too. Couldn't help it. Being alone and watching a good man living a good life totally devoted to his family had a way of making a woman fall for his spirit when hers was tender. Made a woman compare her own mistakes and bad choices in men to Rick, and he won hands down every time. They didn't make men like that anymore. But no woman should let herself fall in love with a man who has his heart held down tight by another woman. That would always end badly.

Grace did love him, she always had. Just wasn't meant to be, so she settled with hope and optimism, only to wind up alone and heartbroken living for the moments when Rick's load brought him this way and he walked through the Denny's door. He was always in a good mood with good things to say. Grace would never tell him, and she knew he didn't feel the same way and never would. She would just have to be content being his friend.

"Whatcha doing tonight?" asked Anne as she wrapped silverware by the cash register. It was three in the afternoon, and Denny's was experiencing a slow Tuesday for a change.

"Watching TV with the kids," Grace responded. "It's spaghetti night. *Stranger Things* on Netflix, I think that's what they said. Sadie is going to make cookies."

Grace's nine-year-old loved cooking, and cookies were her thing. Grace was looking forward to being with her kids. Her day off was tomorrow. She planned on doing laundry and getting some things done around the house. Pay some bills, go to the bank and the grocery store. Tonight was all about the kids. Thank God she was on the day shift now, and the kids were older.

Life was so much easier. Seemed like they could see each other more. Grace got to go to all the games the kids participated in now.

"What about yourself?" Grace asked Anne.

"Well, I thought about grilling some steaks for me and the old man, Tom, from next door," Anne said.

Tom was Anne's neighbor. There was a budding romance going on there. Grace just knew it. Anne was in her sixties and still working. Looked and acted like a teenager and had the heart of an angel.

Grace just hoped Tom had good intentions. Grace didn't know too much about Tom, but she knew Anne was attracted to him. Had been since Tom moved in next door about a month ago. Good looking, single, sixty-year-olds were hard to find, and one had landed right in Anne's lap. She was seizing that opportunity given to her with everything she had.

Later that night after the kids had gone to bed, Grace lay thinking about what the future might bring. She had a simple life. She had struggles, but so did everyone. She loved her kids. She was thankful that God had blessed her with three beautiful children. They were what she lived for. Yes, one day it would be nice to share her life with someone, but for right now she had a job to do. To raise her kids, give them a good life. That was her duty. She was determined to do her best.

Rick

Rick had been thinking about his dad lately.

Rick's father, Thurman, was anointed to preach—yes, he was, and chased by the devil at the same time. He sure could bring a crowd to its feet. He also had slept with a good thirty percent of his female congregation. They were not telling. He sure wasn't. He'd go home convicted, fast for days and pray for forgiveness, then give into temptation the next chance he got. He was a troubled man.

When Rick's mother, Diane, found out after 18 years of marriage, she walked to the barn and shot herself in the head with a .38 Smith and Wesson that Thurman kept in his bedside drawer.

Rick remembered sitting at the kitchen table with his little sister, Lori, and eating grilled cheese sandwiches and Campbell's tomato soup their mother had prepared for them for lunch before she went out the door. The shot rang out loud and strong. Rick could still hear it. He could still feel the emptiness and loneliness that shot had left in his heart.

Diane had suffered from depression, and finding out about the affairs was too much for her troubled mind to handle. She didn't know how.

* * *

Rick remembered holding his little sister's hand at the funeral and telling her everything was going to be all right. Well, it wasn't.

Three months later, Thurman remarried. Delores had two daughters of her own, and they hated little Lori. They tolerated Rick. Rick was a big help to his father, which meant Lori was at home fending for herself.

Thurman also owned a successful convenience store, Lucky's Mini Market. Rick worked there every day after school—stocking, cleaning, taking out the trash. The family had named the store after a dog that they had rescued from the side of the road one Saturday as they were passing through. Ended up taking it to a local vet because its leg was injured. That's why they had stopped initially, because the dog was limping. The dog had taken an instant liking to Lori, so they put him in the station wagon and stopped to get Lucky some medical attention.

After dropping off the dog at the vet's and getting recommendations for lunch, they had set off walking through the town and exploring. Rick's dad had fallen in love with the town. They all had. They ended up eating at Luke's Café, and that's when Rick's dad had found out the small town was in need of a preacher.

After lunch, they went back to pick up the dog with intentions to stay.

"He sure is lucky," the vet said. "Nothing wrong with him that time won't fix. The leg isn't broken, just bruised."

He had been right. Lucky lived another 12 years. It had been a good day for the entire family, as well as the new addition.

* * *

Rick tried the best that he could to comfort and protect Lori, but once he turned eighteen, Rick joined the Army. That left sixteen-year-old Lori pretty much on her own. Lori wrote back and forth. Rick called when he could.

Lori left home two months after Rick left to live with their Aunt Rosalie. Rosalie was their mom's little sister who had lived in Columbus, Ohio at the time. Lori and Rick had discussed the move after Rosalie offered to let Lori move in, and they had decided it was the best thing to do. Aunt Rosalie owned a small restaurant and left it to Lori when she died. Lori still runs it today. It's called Diane's Diner. Lori has a small chain of them now spread across Ohio.

* * *

When Rick got out of the Army, he met a Bible College student in a bar. He was fresh out of the Army and looking for the next chapter. She was trying to save lost souls, and there he was. Her name was Lisa.

Pretty as a button, tiny little thing. Biggest thing about her were those beautiful green eyes. She had soft brown hair, a sweet smile, and a gentle voice. Rick fell hard. Lisa was introducing herself, talking about God. He didn't have the heart to tell her he already had a relationship with God, and it was damaged. He and God were taking a break. His choice, not God's. Of course, later, he did explain about his father and mother's deaths. She seemed to understand completely.

He had been distant from God for a long while now, and here he was, falling in love with one of God's biggest cheerleaders. God really does have a sense of humor.

* * *

Rick and Lisa got married seven months later in Lexington, Kentucky where they had met so that Lisa could finish college, and then they would start a family. Rick bought a truck and worked for Lisa's dad. Lisa's dad owned a long-haul trucking company. They hauled everything from toilet paper to truck parts and everything in between. Rick would work for him for a while. They had a pretty good plan.

They bought a little house with two spare rooms. Rick planned to go back to school eventually on the Army's dime, and he had saved quite a bit. He used some of that for the down payment on the house. Lisa wanted to change the world and make it a better place. She had done a fine job with him so far.

* * *

Lisa had a light around her. Being in her presence healed a man. Rick had felt the melting away almost at once. A release, a calm. Lisa had a gift.

She eventually got a job as a social worker, moving on to the foster system program.

She met and fell in love with three special young boys. They were brothers. Their parents had died in a car accident. They were going to be separated. Lisa couldn't bear to think of them not being together, so she asked some friends in the system for help, and Lisa brought the boys home. Scott, Steve, and John were Rick and Lisa's only children. They brought them so much joy. The boys were twelve, eight, and six when Rick and Lisa officially became their parents.

Scott and Steve shared a room, and John had his own room. It was the smallest, and he was the smallest.

It made sense. It all worked out. They used John's room as an office. They did. Rick guesses, one day, he will again. He hasn't thought that far ahead. He was just going through the motions right now. He knew he could never sell the place. The memories were hard, but he could never let go completely. He did not want to move on.

* * *

When you're in the truck all alone, your mind wanders, sometimes in the future, sometimes in the past, Rick thought. *I'm concentrating on the past these days.* Rick has had some good memories to get him through the past few months. The summers. The vacations. Camping and fishing with the boys. Long talks on the front porch, staring into the night and talking about the welfare of the boys, holding hands, Lisa in one rocker and Rick in the other only a few inches away.

It was their favorite time together. The only time they usually got alone on a day-to-day basis was listening to the night sounds, feeling joyful and content—just the two of them. Talking about having grandkids one day. The places they would take them. Family dinners getting bigger. That reminded Rick he needed to call Scott and check on his wife.

* * *

Laney was pregnant, and the baby was due in four months. Lisa would have been so excited and would have been right there in the delivery room. She would've made the best grandmother. It was another girl for the two of them. When Scott and Laney had met, Laney had a two-year-old daughter named Kaylynn, and Scott had made such a good dad right from the very start. Kaylynn was four years old now and excited about her little sister.

Rick pulled into the Pilot and finished up his logbook, preparing for the next day. As always when he finished for the day, he placed his right forefinger to his lips, then placed his finger on the photo he kept on his visor of Lisa and the boys.

"Goodnight, darling, I love you," he said aloud.

Lowdown

Rick was going into the Denny's after paying for fuel Tuesday evening. On the way in, he saw an older man sitting in a wheelchair. Rick had seen him a couple of times sitting under an old oak tree off to the side of the property where travelers sat and ate lunch at one of the available picnic tables, and occasionally walked their dogs. A pretty spot. A soft breeze seemed to be a normal occurrence in this area. Grace had told Rick the regulars called the man "Lowdown," in reference to the chair, Rick guessed.

As Rick ordered his usual cheeseburger, he picked up an extra. Had the two bags in one hand and two diet cokes juggled between the other. They were out of Pepsi in cans today, and Coke was on sale two for one, so why not? Rick only drank from cans, so he couldn't always get what he preferred. Coke was good. Hoped it was good for his friend. As he approached Lowdown, he noticed the older man studying him. Very few people knew anything about Lowdown. One person who knew him was Monroe West, but no one knew much about him either.

Monroe owned the adjacent lot. He had a building on it that used to be a dry cleaners turned office building. Now it was home to Lowdown. Monroe had kept the cable on for Lowdown. The place had a small bath and kitchen area too. Lowdown liked to talk to people and study them. You can learn a lot about people that way. Most people think he is homeless, and they give him money sometimes. He takes it. He ain't no fool. Keeps it in an oil can. There's over two thousand dollars or more in there. He's keeping it for a rainy day. You just never know when the rain comes. You just never know what a man has, and what a man hasn't got. It shouldn't matter, but most people are impressed by what a man has.

Rick wasn't. He thought he was helping a man down on his luck, offering friendship and maybe lunch.

Rick sat down on the highwall next to the man.

"Whatcha got there?" said the man to Rick.

"A couple of burgers," Rick said. "Pretty good ones. Would you like one?"

"Sure would. They smell pretty good, don't they?"

"Yes, sir, they do."

"Thank you."

"Pretty day out," Rick said as he handed his new friend a hamburger, then began to unwrap his own.

"Yes, it's been a nice day to people watch," the man said. "I enjoy it. Enjoy the thinking too. You're right, by the way. The burger is a good one."

Rick held out his hand. "My name is Rick."

"You can call me Hank," said the man, shaking Rick's outstretched hand.

"Well, Hank, I am running late today. Some days are like that, I guess. Nothing has been on time for me today, so I thought I would just sit down for a while and eat. Normally I do it while I'm driving. It gets a little messy sometimes."

Rick didn't ask the man why he was out here in a wheelchair. Thought that if he wanted to explain, he would.

"So, how long have you been trucking?" Hank asked.

"About 30 years," Rick replied.

"That's a long time to be doing anything. You married?"

"I was."

The man sensed he should drop that line of questioning. "Got any kids?"

"Three boys, one granddaughter, and another one on the way," Rick said.

The two men talked for about an hour. They talked about politics. Rick found out Hank had been in the Army as well. They talked about that for a while. Hank had been in a wheelchair about six months. He was in a bad car accident. The doctor said that, with time, he would recover with therapy.

"Healing takes longer when you get older," Hank said. "At first, I didn't try. My friend talked me into going to a doctor friend of his. Now I'm seeing improvement. I'm hopeful."

After a while, Rick got up, walked to his right, and picked some small wildflowers.

"Are those for me?" Hank laughed.

"No," said Rick. "They are for my butterfly."

"Your butterfly?" Hank thought maybe he didn't hear him right.

"Yes, it's the darndest thing," said Rick, and he told Hank the story about how the butterfly had stayed with him for a few days now.

"You're kidding me," Hank said.

"No, sir. I leave and get gas and go in and stay for over thirty minutes sometimes, and she is still there. If she is gone, she always pops back in before I pull out. I promised my granddaughter I'd keep flowers for Willow in the truck. I have a mason jar. I put a little bottled water in there. She lands on it from time to time. I was telling my granddaughter about her on the phone the other day, and now every time I call my son, she gets on the phone and asks me if I've given Willow her fresh flowers for the day."

"Willow?"

"That's what I named her," Rick said, half embarrassed. It did sound different when you told a grown man about it out loud.

Hank didn't say what he was thinking. He just laughed and laughed.

"I've got a name I'm going to stick on you!" Hank said. "The Butterfly Man."

Rick laughed, "Yes, I guess I am at that."

Scott

Scott Morgan was a thirty-two-year-old Volvo mechanic instructor at the local community college. It was a new program brought into the area, and he was fortunate enough to have been the one chosen for the job, out of over 200 applicants.

Scott had been adopted by Rick and Lisa Morgan when he was twelve years old. He had learned everything he knew about being a mechanic from Rick. Almost every Saturday, he and Rick would work all day on a vehicle of some sort. The Dodge, the Kenworth, Scott's Camaro. That is how they got to know each other in the beginning.

One Saturday about three months after the boys had moved in with Rick and Lisa, Scott and Rick were changing oil in the Dodge. Seventies music was playing in the background. Scott remembered asking Rick a question that had been on his mind.

"Do you believe that there is a God?"

Rick thought for a moment before he answered.

"Yes, son, I do," Rick said. "I don't pretend to understand him, though."

"Do you pray to God?" Scott continued.

"I do, and I try to read the Bible every day."

Rick promised his mother he would as a child. She always reminded him until it became a habit. One of the many good ones that he had. He had come away from reading the Bible with more questions than answers, but of course he did not say that to Scott. Better that Scott figures that out on his own.

"Do you love God?" The questions kept coming.

Rick said, "I try to do the right thing. I think that is what God wants from us. I want to feel like I did as good as I possibly could each day. The important thing is to keep trying."

Rick was relieved when Scott moved on to the task at hand. Scott cranked up the radio in the Kenworth and turned some bolts.

Scott laughed now at that memory. They had discussed that moment years later, on the front steps one morning while having a cup of coffee when Scott had stopped by to introduce Laney to his parents.

Scott had been blessed with the best parents. He and his brothers had been loved by special people, and even though they were not related biologically, the three boys looked just like Rick Morgan. Tall, sandy blond hair, blue eyes. Acted like him too. Good boys, tried to be the best at everything they did. Kind and hard working.

The boys really admired Rick, and part of the reason they turned out so well was that they wanted Rick to be proud of them. And he was; they never doubted it. They'd had a good mom, too. Scott missed her so much. Their mom was always the one to take them to church when she could get them all to go.

Sometimes, Lisa gave up and went by herself. You could bet big money that because of that missed Sunday, they all three would go the next Sunday, for sure. They always prayed before meals. Bedtime prayers, always. Lost the fight with Christian music in the car, though. You win some, you lose some.

Scott laughed out loud.

"I just want you to know your options," she would say. "That you are not alone. You always have Jesus."

She let it go and started singing to whatever was playing on the radio.

Man, we had good parents, Scott thought.

Had, past tense. His dad was having a hard time right now, but Scott knew the man Rick was, and he would find his way.

Lisa

L isa Morgan was dying, and she knew it. She wasn't ready to tell her husband or her boys. She wanted to spare them that pain for as long as she could. She had kept this secret from them for six months. It was getting harder. For a good Christian girl, she sure had turned out to be quite the little liar.

She had never kept secrets from Rick, and it wasn't fair, but she wasn't ready to shatter their world, which was also hers, so some of it was selfish. Sometimes it was easier to deal with alone. Once it was out there, she would have emotions to deal with other than her own. She wasn't ready.

* * *

She fell in love with Rick at first sight, in a bar of all places. She remembered it well. The image of that first moment was still vivid in her tired mind. Blue eyes and a big, sweet smile. Blue jeans and a Packers baseball cap. An old, scruffy pair of Ariat boots that had seen better days. Rick still had them.

He was drinking a beer, sitting on a stool at the bar like he was waiting for her to show up.

They started up a conversation, hit it off, and never looked back. Rick was the kind of man a woman wanted. Loyal, kind, patient, and encouraging. The kind of man that had your back when you weren't there. The kind of man you wanted to marry and have your babies with. He was the one for Lisa. She fell hard.

It was disappointing when they could not have kids of their own. But God brought those three boys to them, and she knew it. They'd had such a joyful life together. Fishing, camping, boy scouts, football. They had tried to go to the movies at least once a week. Rick and Lisa never knew time alone after that. They were having such a good time raising those boys that they never even thought of needing it. Very seldom were they ever separated.

Then the boys grew up, went to college, and met girls, of course. The girls just blended in with the activities that they always enjoyed. All three boys went to local colleges, so they usually came home for weekends, or she and Rick would travel to whichever college, and they would all meet up. Either way, Lisa would end up doing three sets of laundry. She loved taking care of her boys. She was so glad the boys were in good relationships.

Lisa worried about Rick. She knew in time he would rebound because of the boys, but he would take her news hard.

Lori

Lori Morgan had known her share of heartache, like most people, but overall she had led a good life.

Running a business was hard work, but she loved everything about it. Right now, the fifty-three-year-old, blue-eyed blonde was sitting in the back office with her booted feet resting on the corner of the old desk her aunt had used for over 30 years. Thinking of her aunt brought tears to Lori's eyes. She was also thinking about her brother, Rick. Lori never married. She'd had a great role model in Rick and Lisa. They'd had the best marriage Lori had ever seen. Lori missed Lisa too. Lisa had always been so sweet to Lori.

Lori was worried about Rick. It was time for their weekly call.

Last week, Rick had been telling her some wild story about a butterfly living in the Kenworth with him. After his sense of humor returned, she was going to have to tell that story at Thanksgiving dinner. They would have a big laugh over that. Lori would make sure of it. Laughing at Rick was a family favorite.

Rick always gave them plenty to work with. She and Rick had a rocky few years as kids. Rick had always been there for her, though. He was like Batman. He always showed up when she needed him. He always saved the day. He was her hero and her best friend. He gave great advice, and she needed some right now.

* * *

Lori had met someone, Jeff, and he'd asked her to go on a family vacation with his entire family.

It would be a couple of weeks at the beach with his mom, dad, and two girls. His parents had a house in Myrtle Beach. She didn't know if she was ready. She would have to leave her restaurant. Lori had a great staff, but it was a busy time. She hadn't been on a vacation in five years. This was a big deal, meeting Jeff's family.

She had met Jeff at the restaurant. He and his family owned the local company that supplied paper products for her restaurant and other assorted necessities.

Lori picked up the phone and called her big brother, the Butterfly Man. She laughed.

"Hey, trouble," Rick said on the third ring.

"Hey, big brother. How's it going?" Lori replied.

"Pretty good, I guess. Still trucking up and down the road. Making a living. With gas prices the way they are, it's making it hard on a man buying diesel the way I do. Good to hear your voice. Been thinking about you today. How proud I am of you. Is the restaurant still raking in the big bucks? I thought of taking a road trip and coming up to see you for a couple of weeks."

"You're kidding," Lori said. "This couldn't be more perfect."

Lori explained the situation.

"Well, I have some time off coming up, and I'm not ready to go home yet, so I could ride up to see you and get me a good meal or two," Rick said.

"So, will you?" Lori asked with excitement in her voice. Her mind had been made up. It was a sign.

"Count me in," Rick said. "You need a vacation, and I need somewhere to go."

Rick and Hank

Every Fourth of July, Rick's hauling outfit shut down for two weeks. Rick had been thinking of going to see his sister, Lori. He was not ready to go home. Going to his post office and paying his bills was painful enough. All the questions. Everyone and everything he saw reminded him of Lisa, and he just wanted to get out of town as fast as he could. Thank goodness they didn't have any animals to take care of. He could just grieve alone and try to get through this. He remembered to mail his neighbor a check for mowing. Rick stopped at the local Walmart to pick up a few things he might need for the trip.

* * *

He and Hank had been talking a lot lately. Hank had been doing his therapy, and it was beginning to go pretty well. Rick asked Hank if he was up for a road trip, and Hank said yes. Rick would run by the Pilot and pick Hank up around six. They would stop by Denny's and pick up burgers for the road.

Lori had been okay with Hank tagging along. Everything was all set. Rick was glad for the company, and Hank seemed excited. It was a good situation for the three of them, and Hank had some experience with cooking. He and his wife had owned a restaurant. It was the family business. Very successful.

As they were driving along, Hank laughed and said, "Well, I'm surprised you didn't bring your little friend."

Rick knew he was talking about the butterfly.

"She was there when I left," Rick said. "I thought about bringing her, but I figured you would make fun of me, and I didn't want to put her through the rejection." Rick laughed before continuing, "I left the window down a bit and put some fresh flowers in her jar. That was the first thing Kaylynn said to me this morning when I told her I was going to see Aunt Lori. I always keep my promises to my girl."

"Yeah, right," said Hank. Hank knew Rick would have left flowers anyway without being reminded. That was just the way he was. He was tender hearted towards all creatures, including himself.

Hank was glad he didn't have to share shotgun with a butterfly, though.

Rick didn't know if Willow was the same butterfly he had started off with. Sometimes she looked different, but it didn't matter. He was committed now. A butterfly of some sort found its way into the cab of his truck from time to time. That's all Rick knew, and because of his connection to butterflies, he'd do the best he could to keep them coming. They brought him comfort, and he found himself looking for them when he got in the truck.

Rick was looking forward to this trip. He was going to look after the restaurant for Lori while she was away, as well as see to some repairs she needed done around the house and three of the restaurants. Rick already had a list started in his head of things he would need to pick up at Lowe's before they got to the house.

Rick loved this sort of work. It had been a while. The weather was going to be good for the next few days, too. Perfect time to get outdoor projects done. He spent most of his time sitting in the truck. He enjoyed working with his hands outside on a sunny day. Loved the feeling of being helpful and looking back on a job well done with pride. This time, he had an assistant along for the ride.

This was going to be a nice time for him and Hank.

Lori could have hired someone else to do the work, he guessed, but she liked the way Rick did things, and she knew Rick would enjoy doing it.

Hank

Hank was thinking back on the last year. He was on a road trip with his friend, Rick Morgan. The radio was playing in the background. Both men were tired, and it was past midnight. But they had decided to push forward, get up early, and start on that list. Both men had grown quiet, entertaining themselves now with their own thoughts. Hank's thoughts were on Claire Davis.

Claire and Hank had been a great team in everything they did. Everyone, including Hank, thought that the two of them had a good, solid marriage. One night at a mutual friend's birthday celebration, Hank had found out that he had been wrong. Claire admitted to being in love with someone else. Hank was stunned. He hadn't seen this coming. He hadn't seen the car coming at them from the passenger side on their drive home, either. Claire was killed instantly, and Hank spent the next three months in the hospital.

Hank still struggled with unanswered questions. He had been unable to talk with Claire. He didn't know who the guy she was in love with was or how long they had been seeing each other.

Rehab was a slow process for Hank. He wasn't fighting for his life back. Hank wasn't motivated to get his life back. He had no life to go back to, not the one he thought he had. He and Claire didn't have children. She did not want children and that had been enough for him. So, now what? Hank was grieving, but not over Claire's death as much as he was grieving over losing the Claire he thought she was. She had destroyed that image.

* * *

Hank's half-brother, Monroe, had let him stay in an old office building he used back before retirement.

Hank had been hiding out. After getting discharged, with orders to come back twice a week, Hank wanted to be where no one knew him so that he could lick his wounds and heal both mentally and physically. There had been an old wheelchair in the back of the office in storage. Hank had sat down in the chair and just stayed there. It hurt to walk, it hurt to think, it hurt to feel. The chair became his place of solace. Hank didn't have a rocker on the front porch, or a front porch, so he improvised. Sitting in that chair had become therapeutic in many ways. It reminded him that he very well could've ended up in one. So, when he saw the chair, he dusted it off with the back of his hand and propped his tired, old body into it.

Hank would do his exercises the physical therapist sent home with him. He didn't get out much for about six weeks. Monroe came to see him and to bring him supplies. One day, he wheeled himself right out the back door of the office, just fooling around, and found himself parking next door to the Pilot. He was watching people, watching traffic, and slowly healing over the next few weeks. He looked forward to the conversations he had with Rick. Hank found himself opening up a little, forming a friendship. Here he was, on his way to Ohio, with his new friend. Hank looked forward to the week ahead.

Rick and Hank

Rick was getting tired. He had been driving for over five hours now. He stopped a couple of times, but for the most part, he was driving and talking to Hank. They had fallen into silence about twenty minutes back.

Rick looked over to his right. Hank was 65 years old, slim, ex-Army intelligence. Worked out every day until about six months ago, and he was in way better shape than Rick at ten years his junior.

Hank was intelligent and always wore a baseball cap. Rick kidded him that it was to cover his bald head. Hank wore army green almost always. Hank said he just liked the color.

One more hour, and they would be there. Lori had left a house key and more directions under the front door mat. She said, "Leave me a message and let me know when you get there. Love you."

Rick's texted response was, "Same here. Love you too."

* * *

Rick and Hank worked all day. Home repairs, a water leak, a crumbling step, garage door. Mostly repairs on the old house. The restaurants appeared to be in pretty good shape—the two they had gotten around to, anyway. By day two, all six had been checked on. Good food was supplied at all six, and it was on the house. Boss's orders. No argument from Hank or Rick on that one.

* * *

Day two was coming to a close. Lori had called earlier. She was taking a road trip, having some much-needed time alone, just her and her '67 Impala. That car was the love of her life. It was a nice ride. Rick drove it once for ten minutes, then Lori took it back from him, and no one had driven it since. She should be meeting up with Jeff in the morning. She let Rick know where she was staying tonight. She had added a stop to look at some tile for the restaurant at a place she had heard about from a customer. So, a slight detour in the morning.

* * *

Rick and Hank played a game of Rummy to 500, then watched one of Rick's favorite movies that was playing on cable, part one of *Lonesome Dove*. They had eaten dinner at home tonight. Hank grilled a couple of steaks while they were waiting on the second coat of paint to dry on the spare room in the back. Then, they would be moving the furniture back in. The to-do list was growing shorter.

It felt good to do some physical work. Having Hank around to help and to carry on with made the work easier and way more enjoyable. Rick was feeling good about what they had accomplished.

Rick could hear Hank working with the shower head in the main bathroom in the back of the house. Hank volunteered to do the plumbing. Rick had not put up much of a fuss. Rick did the bulk of the paint jobs. Rick liked that kind of work. He would have liked to do that full time. A new paint job made everything look brand new.

Lisa always said she loved the smell of fresh paint. They had changed the color of every room in the house several times over the years. Rick had enjoyed the work—not so much the color choices, though. He loved making Lisa and the boys as happy and as comfortable as he could, whatever that entailed, including working on cars for the boys. Colors had changed several times over the years on those, too.

Lori's house could use a paint job on the outside, but it was doubtful he and Hank could accomplish that job on this trip. Maybe on the next trip.

* * *

Rick woke up to the sound of his cell phone. He had fallen asleep on the sofa watching TV.

"Hello," Rick said. He was prepared to hear Lori's voice checking in.

"Is this Rick Morgan?" Rick didn't recognize the voice.

"Yes, it is," Rick replied.

"This is Jeff Hamlin," the voice said. "Lori's friend. She gave me your number. She hasn't called me to check in like she promised to do, and I am getting worried. Have you heard from her tonight?"

Rick quickly checked his phone for messages, then said, "No, nothing. Let me call her and I will call you right back."

Rick disconnected the call with Jeff and immediately called his sister. No answer.

Lori

"Ouch," Lori said out loud.

She couldn't see. Her head was hurting and bleeding. She had felt something sticky in her hair and left side of her face as her fingers rubbed gently against her skin. It was dark and cold. She was sitting on hard ground. She tried to stand up. She was a little bit shaky.

She was in her pajamas and her house shoes were missing.

The last thing she remembered was that she had left her purse in her car. After taking a shower, she walked to where she had parked her car at the back of the hotel to retrieve it. She felt a hard hit to the head and had come to wherever this is. No keys, no purse, no cell.

She was so thirsty. A diet Dr. Pepper over ice would be good right now. Like the one she had waiting for her in her room.

The first thing she needed to do was to get out of here. Her eyes were adjusting to her surroundings.

Wait until she told Rick about this one. Hopefully he would get her out of this mess like all the other times. Jeff must be so worried. She was going to call them both right after she got out of the shower, but discovered her missing purse, which had her cell in it.

Light began to peek through openings in the wall. So, she was in a barn, Lisa thought. Hopefully there would be a house nearby. She needed to find the door.

"Ouch."

Her bare feet had stepped on something sharp protruding from the floor. She added a good pair of shoes to her growing list of items needed. All she needed was to get to a phone.

She liked having direction. It was keeping her panic down. She made a promise to herself that someone was going to pay for this, one way or another. She hoped her car was okay.

It was growing light outside, which enabled her to find the door, and it was a total surprise when it opened easily.

She saw a house up ahead, and that is where she headed as fast as her condition permitted.

Rick, Jeff, and Hank

Rick and Hank headed South as fast as the old Dodge would permit. They were meeting Jeff at the hotel where Lori had been staying. Jeff had contacted the local police station and called Rick back to say that they'd arrived on the scene somewhere near Travelers Rest, South Carolina.

The night manager had let them in her room, and there had been no evidence of foul play. They were looking at video surveillance. Jeff would call back as soon as he found out anything.

Rick was thinking about what a good girl Lori had always been. Smart as a whip and as loyal as a cocker spaniel to her big brother, Rick. They had always been there for each other. They had such a strong bond brought on by a complicated upbringing. They were abandoned by the grownups, so they took up all the slack for each other. They were the stronger for it.

Rick didn't know what was happening to his little sister, but he knew that he needed her to be okay. He couldn't lose another person in his life. He started to pray.

Hank was praying for his friend's situation too. He hadn't known Rick long, but he knew that his friend was worried and hurting, and he prayed everything would be okay.

The phone rang, startling both men.

It was Lori's number that Rick saw as he picked up the phone.

"Hello?"

Lori and Katherine

Lori walked slowly across the soft grass to the old, white farmhouse in the middle of the field that she found herself in.

Lori knocked on the door. She had no idea what time it was. She and Rick never wore watches. Like everyone else, now they glanced at their phones when they wanted to know the time.

Lori did not know what to expect when she knocked on the door, but it was certainly not this. A nice-looking woman in her sixties opened the door. She had long, blonde hair and was wearing it well. She was dressed in blue jeans and a denim button down, with wire-rimmed glasses, and she was pointing a 22 shotgun skillfully at Lori.

"What can I do for you?" said the woman in a soft, even voice.

"I need your help," Lori said. She continued to explain as best as she could what had happened. She couldn't remember much. Took two minutes. The woman laid the gun to the side.

"Come in please," the woman said. "I apologize for the treatment, but you never know out here."

Lori went into the house. The first thing she asked for was a phone. She called Rick. Then Jeff. The woman gave Lori her address. All three men were headed her way, along with the police. The women had time for a cup of tea and oatmeal cookies.

The woman's name was Katherine Cooper. Her husband died about a year ago, and she was out here all by herself in this big, old house. Katherine had been a local cop with her husband for over twenty years.

She knew the cops that showed up with Jeff.

Lori told the police everything she knew, which wasn't much. They informed her that they had the whole thing on video thanks to the hotel night manager.

A young boy had hit her over the head, placed her in the trunk of the car, and apparently dropped her off here. She was two miles from the crime scene. It looked like the boy was after the car. It could have been so much worse.

The cops left with the promise of updates as soon as they could regarding the whereabouts of the Impala, as well as the identity of the kid. Hopefully, the kid would supply suitable explanations.

Rick and Hank showed up after the cops left. Introductions were made. Rick's hug took the breath right out of Lori.

Jeff wanted to take Lori to the ER. Hank and Rick followed Jeff and Lori there.

Katherine followed in her black Volvo SUV that looked like it had been around for a while. Her license plate read, Not2day.

After everything checked out, Katherine invited everyone to come back to the house to have lunch and to stay the night if needed.

Lori had taken a shower earlier, and Katherine bandaged Lori's feet and cleaned them as best she could. Katherine also cleaned the injury on Lori's head. The doctor had said that Katherine did a fine job. She had given Lori a change of clean clothes and shoes. Lori was actually feeling okay.

Everyone agreed to take Katherine up on her offer. The group was mentally tired, driving through the night with no sleep. Rick was so relieved that this situation had ended as well as it did.

They all had a lot to be thankful for.

Rick and Katherine

The crew woke up five hours later, give or take one at a time, to the amazing smell of coffee, biscuits and gravy, and other assorted goodies Katherine had graciously prepared. Just what the doctor ordered.

Katherine was explaining what the next plan in her life was as everyone gathered around the table, and Rick could not believe it. She and her husband had wanted to turn this big, old house into a home for boys. The same dream he and Lisa had once upon a time.

Katherine's husband had been a foster kid, and he wanted to do what his parents had done for him. Show them how to build a new life from a not-so-perfect one. Rick had become an instant fan of the man he would never get to meet.

Katherine was saying, "I haven't had a family around this table in such a long time. This feels good. I hate like the dickens what happened to you, Lori, but I am so glad that we got to meet each other."

"Agreed," said Lori, looking around the table at all the sweet faces. She felt blessed for sure.

It had been decided. Lori and Jeff would join Jeff's family and finish out the vacation that they had planned. Lori promised Rick to take it easy.

Rick and Hank would stick around and wait for information on the car. They would stay with Katherine one more day. She had insisted. The breakfast Katherine served was the deciding factor, and they all knew it. Plus, Rick was interested in Katherine's plans for her house. Rick had some ideas he would like to share with Katherine that he and Lisa always talked about, not too long ago.

* * *

He and Lisa had enjoyed raising the boys so much that they made plans to do it again once the boys started college. They were out on the front porch, sitting in their rockers as part of their nightly ritual, and discussing the future after the boys left home.

Rick noticed Katherine had some rocking chairs on her front porch as he went out to the truck that morning. It was a nice home. Well maintained. It could be the perfect home for children to grow up in under the right guidance. The house had a good feel to it. It was peaceful and uncomplicated. Two good ingredients for raising strong and content children.

* * *

Rick and Hank said their goodbyes with a promise to return for supper after they took care of some business for Lori. Rick was determined to find his sister's car, and when Rick Morgan was determined, look out.

Jesse

Jesse was sitting in a juvenile detention center office, waiting on Sharon Kiser to come back into the room, and to tell him what the future had in store for him. Jesse was one week away from turning eighteen. He was a nice-looking kid. Had a chip on his shoulder. His parents had died in a car accident when he was ten years old, and he had been adopted by Chris and Peggy Fridley. He was just waiting to turn eighteen so that he could leave and be out on his own.

They had been good to him. He just never felt a connection. They were not his family. Jesse was not like his foster parents or the kids his age. He was a quiet, solitary young man. Small in stature. He lived to read. He had always used books to escape the real world, to explore other possibilities. He never left home without one. Even now he had a copy of *Wuthering Heights* in his jacket pocket. It was small paperback version given to him by a cute girl in his English class. It wasn't what he usually read, but he really liked the writing style of Emily Brontë. He probably wouldn't share that information ever. Plus, he was hoping to have a conversation about the novel with the giver. He had to read it just in case.

Sharon Kiser walked into the room with a flourish and a big smile on her face.

"Well, Jesse, this must be your lucky day," she said. "Lori Morgan is not pressing charges. Because of your age and your foster parents speaking on your behalf to the authorities, you, my friend, are off the hook. It didn't hurt that your parents are good friends with the local judge."

Jesse didn't know what to say. He just nodded and stood up. "So, does that mean that I can go now?"

"Yes, your parents are finishing up with some paperwork, and soon they will be able to take you home. Jesse, you are a lucky young man."

Sharon reached out her right hand to shake Jesse's.

Jesse reached out his hand and spoke, "Thank you."

"Take care of yourself," Sharon said and turned to leave the room.

* * *

Jesse was relieved of course, but now he would have to explain why he did this to Chris and Peggy. Jesse really didn't know how to explain it. He just wanted to leave. To start a new life on his own terms. He should not have taken the car. Hurting the lady and hiding her in the barn just happened. His plan was to go somewhere new, anywhere, to be someone else. Maybe drive a few hours until he ran out of gas.

He was going to leave the car on the side of the road. Walk to a nearby town. Get a job and start over. Then the owner of the car showed up, and his simple plan took a wrong turn really fast. He panicked in a moment of indecision and desperation. The two of them had fought over the keys. They both tripped, and when the lady's head hit the front bumper, she fell to the ground.

Looking back, what he should have done was to have repaired the motor in his own car and tell his parents that he wanted to leave. That would have been the sensible thing to do, but they would have argued and talked him out of it. They wanted him to go to college. They had a plan.

* * *

Jesse wanted a clean break. No ties to his foster parents, and no ties to the parents that had put him in a position to be adopted in the first place. He was angry. Irrationally so, maybe. He resented being handed over to complete strangers, left on his own at the age of ten to do the best with what had been given to him.

* * *

He had woken up to social workers in the middle of the night trying to explain what happened to his parents. They were hit by a drunk driver. Jesse was told to pack a few things, because he was being transferred to a foster house since there was no one else to call on his behalf.

* * *

The decision to run had formed when he saw the car. He was just out for a walk, having every intention of going back home. What he had done was so stupid, he couldn't believe it.

Jesse was brought out of his memories by the sound of movement behind him. Chris and Peggy came towards him. Of course, Peggy was crying. Chris was hugging him and saying, "Son, everything is going to be alright."

Jesse was thinking what a shame it was that he couldn't be content with being a good son to this super nice couple.

Rick

The boy, Jesse, had told the police where he'd left Lori's car. Apparently, the car had run out of gas. The police had picked him up walking toward Horry County, South Carolina. Jesse told the police he hadn't realized Lori was a woman. She had come up behind him. He had turned around with a powerful swing, initially thinking he was protecting himself from a male mugger. They had struggled over the keys, and she had fallen. When he realized what was happening, it was too late; it had happened so fast. He didn't want to leave her laying there, so after checking that she was still breathing, he had taken her to a safe place until she could wake up, near a house where she could walk to for help while giving him time to get away.

Lori talked to Jesse's foster parents.

She hadn't pressed charges, despite the fact that Rick had strongly encouraged her to. Rick was angry at the boy and wanted him to be punished for what he had done. He finally gave in to his little sister's line of reasoning, after Lori ended it with, "That is what Lisa would have wanted us to do. To give the boy a second chance, and forgiveness."

Rick didn't argue with that.

So, he let it go. He and Hank picked up the car, filled it up with gas, and took it to be detailed. Showroom new. Not a scratch on it. At least the kid hadn't damaged the car. Rick looked it over closely.

Rick and Hank were planning to head back to Ohio the next morning to finish up Lori's list before she came home from vacation with Jeff and his family. Lori was having a good time. She had called her big brother last night. She said she was feeling great. She went on and on about how sweet Jeff's girls were, and his parents were so kind. Rick was relieved. He was packing up so that he and Hank could get an early start.

Hank would drive the Dodge and Rick would drive the Impala. He and Hank would be having meatloaf for dinner shortly. Rick could hear laughter coming from the kitchen. Katherine had invited them for a "going-away supper," and Hank had offered to help. When she asked what they wanted, they both replied they'd like meatloaf.

"Meatloaf it is," Katherine had said.

Hank replied, "I used to make a mean meatloaf. It was my great grand-mother Teresa's recipe."

"Well, come on down then, and when you're ready you can help me make supper," Katherine replied with a smile. Hank accepted the offer.

Over dinner, they all talked more about Katherine's plan for a boys home, and Rick shared his and Lisa's idea of wanting to do the same.

"You can still do it, and you can come up any time and see how it's done," Katherine said. "I have some good people in the community with plans to help. Free advice you are welcome to. From what I understand, Lisa sounds like the kind of woman who would have wanted you to con-tinue with these plans."

Katherine continued, "You know, you could do it for her. I think that would make her happy. What's stopping you? I will help as much as I can. Get you in touch with the right people to help you get started."

A timer went off to remind Katherine that she had something in the oven. She stopped and stood up to pull a peach cobbler from the oven.

"South Carolina peaches are the best," Katherine went on. "I am going to send some back with you two before you go. I have a few jars of canned peaches I'll give you, too. I make the best, if I do say so myself."

Rick and Hank agreed that Katherine, in fact, did make the best peach cobbler they ever had. Maybe she was right. South Carolina peaches were the best. They were when she fixed them, anyway.

Later that night, after everyone had long gone to sleep, Rick couldn't stop thinking about conversations he and Lisa had had. Katherine was right. He could still do it. He could get this thing going with a little help, and he had the best place for a boys home—the home he and Lisa had raised their own boys in.

Part Two

Hank

The sun was hot. It was 85 degrees today. There was a soft breeze coming through the trees to cool things down a little, a few seconds at a time. Sure, it felt good. Perfect day for a barbecue.

"I wish this crew would slow down," said Hank. Hank was flipping burgers and adding them to a platter as soon as they were ready. Katherine Cooper, now Hank's wife of over three weeks, gave him a quick kiss as she picked up the platter of burgers to transfer over to a side table, where she, Lori, and Laine were assembling burgers for the boys.

"Boys at this age are hungry all of the time," Katherine laughed as she rushed back to pick up more buns from under the grill table. Katherine and Hank had met last year, and immediately liked each other. Soon after, they fell in love.

Katherine runs a boys home now, just like she and her first husband had always dreamed about doing. Hank serves as her right hand. The boys adore him, and Hank adores the new role as a dad to a bunch of teenage boys.

Hank stopped what he was doing and turned to see his best friend, Rick Morgan, with a cute little blonde, blue-eyed baby on his right hip. Rick walked towards him. Everyone called the baby Lisa. She was named after Rick's dead wife, and she was the main reason Rick was living again. It had been a big year, a good year, filled with healing that change created. A new baby and a new direction for Rick Morgan's life.

Rick had turned his and Lisa's home into a home for boys with the guidance of Katherine and some of Lisa's contacts from when she had worked with foster kids before she died.

Rick had gotten the idea from Katherine. He and Lisa dreamed about doing the same thing with their house when their boys had grown up. Katherine was in the process of doing the same thing to her home, opening it up to boys who needed a good place to grow up.

Since Lisa passed away, Rick had never wanted to go home. He did not want to live in the home that he and Lisa had shared, so with some help from Hank and a few buddies, they transformed the house to accommodate five boys with an extra room for Jesse, who now lived at the house, and an office for staff. The house had turned out just like he and Lisa dreamed it would.

Rick lived in a restored barn on the property. It was solid and clean and had all that he needed. The barn had a shop in the back for working on the various vehicles the boys brought home, and a dozen other projects that they had talked him into doing. Projects Rick would likely never finish, but they were having a good time thinking that they would, and dreaming about what the projects would look like when they finished.

Hank came over once a week to help with the boys. Rick's boys loved Hank too. Hank worked at both homes, changing lives and their small world, making the world a better place for the boys and creating a chance for a better future. That was always the goal. Teaching by example, living a good life, and working together to create healing one day at a time.

Rick had brought over all his boys to Hank and Katherine's today for a barbecue so that they could meet and hopefully have a good time. Grace had driven the donated Suburban over with the five boys. Jesse came over with Lori and her new husband, Jeff.

Lori and Jeff had run off and gotten married one weekend. Lori did not want a big wedding. Jeff did, but Lori always gets what she wants. Jeff was learning that right from the start.

"She looks hungry," Hank said with a laugh, meaning baby Lisa, who now had a few new teeth.

Her birthday was last week. Now, that was a celebration. There had been a party at Rick's, a new puppy, and balloons. Hey, turning one year old was an important birthday.

Baby Lisa reached for a hamburger on a slider bun that Hank had made especially for her little hands. She grabbed it from Hank's outstretched hand and began to nibble immediately. Rick and Hank laughed.

"Yeah, she's hungry," said Rick. "She just had a big cookie five minutes ago. Come to think of it, most of the cookie ended up in the floor of the truck and her car seat. She may have gotten one good bite out of it, so yeah, she could be hungry."

Rick laughed. He sure did love that baby girl, and she loved her Paw Paw Rick. Rick kept her with him every chance he got. Hank was happy for Rick.

"Things settle down any?" Hank asked.

"Yeah, nothing new that I know of," replied Rick.

The men were referring to Jesse's biological father, Dan Jenkins. He had come back looking for his son. Nothing good was gonna come from that, but Rick didn't know how to handle the situation any better than he was doing. Rick had a bad feeling about the man, one that he couldn't explain. But right now, things were calm.

* * *

Dan had showed up late one night when Grace and Matt were working. Grace was Rick's friend from Denny's. Grace had needed a new job, and Rick offered her the position at the house—someone to make dinner and to watch over the boys in the evening.

Rick always had at least two staff members working each shift. Matt Hughes was a history teacher from the local high school. He tutored the boys. He and Grace had met at the house and were currently dating. Rick was happy for them. They worked well together, and the boys loved them both. Grace deserved a good man. Matt seemed kind and patient. He was great with the kids, and everyone told Rick that Matt was the house favorite.

"Well, let me know if I can help," Hank said.

"Thank you, Hank, you know that I will," said Rick.

He hoped that wouldn't be necessary.

Jesse

The man Jesse's mom had been married to wasn't Jesse's biological father. Jesse had been adopted twice.

Jesse's mom became pregnant by a man who had not been interested in the baby she was carrying. Her best friend, David, offered to marry her and loved the thought of raising her baby as his own and had adopted Jesse as soon as he was born.

Eighteen years later, Daniel "Dan" Jenkins showed up at Lisa's home for boys looking for Jess, and explaining that he was his father, and wanted a relationship with his son. He had letters and pictures. Of course, there would have to be a test.

Dan owned a junk yard a couple of hours away and wanted Jess to come down and have lunch and talk to him sometime. Dan had left a card with his cell number on it. An ex-girlfriend had talked him into getting the cards made. She said the cards made the shop look more established. Dan had agreed. Today was the first time Dan used the cards since he had purchased them five years ago.

Jess didn't know if he wanted to talk to Dan Jenkins or not. He had recently run away from his foster parents, who had adopted him shortly after he moved in with them. They were good people he had never felt connected to. They had given him a loving home, had been nothing but kind and supportive. Now, Jess finds out that he has a father who wants to be a part of his life.

* * *

Jess needed to talk to Rick. Rick was not returning home until tomorrow, so he guessed he would have to wait. It was after twelve o'clock, and Rick would no doubt be asleep. Jesse and Rick had become close over the last year. Rick offered him a home and a job and had encouraged him to enroll in the local community college. Rick taught Jess so much and had helped him adjust to his new life. Jess had to admit it was pretty good. Rick was basically a father to Jesse. Then, Dan Jenkins showed up.

* * *

Rick was a truck driver, and he stayed on the road a lot. When he was home, that is where Jess was. He had a room at Rick's, and at the house. Jess stayed at the house as an extra hand when Rick was away from home. Rick knew about Dan's visit, but he and Jess had not discussed the visit in depth. Jess wanted to wait until he could talk to Rick before he made any decisions. He had planned to wait until Rick came home. He had so many questions.

Jess was told that Dan died. None of this made sense to Jess. Why had his mother lied to him? Jess felt like he was missing something, and the only way to get answers was by talking to Dan Jenkins. Jess picked up the phone.

Rick

It was two o'clock in the morning. Rick had just gotten off the phone with Jess. Rick hoped he had helped the boy. It had been late when Jess had called, and Rick was asleep, but he told the boys that he would be available to them at any time, whether he was on the road or not.

Rick had offered to go with Jess to talk to his dad when he got off the road Friday evening, and that seemed to comfort Jess. They had a plan. Rick would wait to form an opinion after he met Dan and had talked to him face to face. Rick's mind went back over the early part of his day before he had to head out and deliver this load.

* * *

The barbecue at Hank's turned out to be a great day for everyone. Hank and Katherine seemed to be settling in with their new roles as husband and wife as well as parents to a bunch of rambunctious teenage boys. There had been lots of laughter and good times today. Healthy memories.

All the boys from both homes participated in the activities and seemed to get along, at least for today.

Rick's sons had all stopped by. Scott and Laine, Kaylynn, and baby Lisa. She always reached for him the minute she caught sight of him or heard his voice. Stevie and John stayed and played a serious game of football with the boys. The boys had made smores right at dark, but Rick had missed that part because he was running late and had to leave for work.

Three of the boys said that they had never made smores before. Well, they could take that memory with them and one day share that memory with their children. The simple moments in life are what you remember and end up doing over and over, because it brought sweet happiness to you, and you want to share it with the people you love and to relive it.

Kaylynn had come up to Rick today, so excited about the butterflies. Rick had planted wildflowers to attract butterflies around the house because Kaylynn loved her Paw Paw's butterfly stories. She, of course, told all the boys the story. They started calling him Butterfly Man too. Rick owned his nickname, and to be honest, he kind of liked it.

He didn't know the life span of a butterfly, but he figured Willow had passed. Either way, she had moved on. He hadn't seen her in the truck for a while now. But every time he saw a butterfly, he thought of Willow. He must have missed Willow, considering all the time and energy he had invested in the flowers—for Kaylynn, of course—to draw her back. Regardless, the flowers made the house look nice, and Lisa would have approved. She also loved flowers.

Before Lisa passed, Rick had gotten in the habit of sending her flowers regularly, especially when he was on the road. He just wanted to let her know he was thinking about her. The last ones he ever sent were spring wildflowers in a white basket. She had said that they were her favorite ones yet. Rick still had them today.

Rick placed the wildflowers in a box along with the basket, and they sat on a shelf in his closet alongside the quilt that his grandmother, Queenie, had made for him when he was born, as well as his favorite gun from his Paw Paw John. The gun was an old 22 rifle that his Paw Paw had taught him how to shoot. That man could drive a nail into a post from 15 yards away from the front porch while sitting in a rocker with that gun.

* * *

Rick was growing tired, so he rolled over and, as always, fell asleep with thoughts of Lisa.

The Boys

At the moment, Lisa's home for boys housed five young men and Jess. He stayed through the week, helping the adults on duty.

* * *

There was William Hayes, a fifteen-year-old, red-headed ball of energy. He had been living with neighbors that his mother had left him with one day. A year later, his grandfather found him and brought him home. His grandfather grew some of the best pot around. He and William had the best time a nine-year-old boy could dream of. No curfews. Potato chips for breakfast. A grandfather who adored him. But, as is often the case, his grandfather was turned in and arrested, and since William had no other relations, he ended up in foster care. That had been a year ago.

William wrote to his grandfather. Rick had promised him that, soon, he would figure out a way to take William to see his grandfather. William wrote that in his last letter. He was waiting for a response. William missed him very much. Funny thing was, his grandfather hated drugs; he never did them, never even tried his own pot. He just got into it to supplement his social security. Taught himself how to make the perfect bud from the internet. People came from all over to buy the good stuff. That is how he got caught. A jealous competitor turned him in.

William lost his way of life. He was adjusting but never gave up hope that he would someday be back with his grandfather, Bradford Hayes.

* * *

David Taylor was a 17-year-old hot head with a big mouth. He loved Rick Morgan and working on cars, and that is where you could always find him. Tinkering and listening to classic rock on the radio that Rick kept on a shelf beside the microwave and the coffee pot. He kept the microwave and coffee pot in the workstation in case they ever ended up working longer and missing dinner. David's favorite food was hot pockets and popcorn, and hot coffee. Rick always made sure he had plenty on hand.

David had been raised by a single parent, Daisey Taylor. She was a dancer. David stayed in the car, a five-year-old silver Lexus, while she worked, doing his homework and taking naps. She didn't want him with a sitter. She didn't trust anyone. She always told him right before she went into the club, "The cat's meow," not to leave the car for any reason.

On her breaks, she would bring him food the other girls had brought for supper. David had cookies and milk every night for dessert. She and her friends would sneak him in on their breaks to use the bathroom and help him with his homework. Bedtime was nine o'clock. She always tucked him in in the backseat and locked the door until around twelve o'clock, when her shift was over. Then they would drive home. One night, she fell asleep behind the wheel and ran into a truck going eighty miles per hour. She was killed instantly.

David was rushed to the hospital. He survived the physical injuries, but mentally he would never be the same. He loved his momma. She had been beautiful, with dark hair and dark eyes, just like David. He missed her and all her friends that helped take care of him. She had tried to keep him close to her and as safe as she could. Society had looked down on Daisey because of what she did for a living, but the other girls had always been good to David and his mother.

They had taken turns reading to him and always reminded him to brush his teeth. Sometimes they made his bed for him in the back seat. Made sure that he had his flashlight and a charged cell phone for emergencies. David still thought of them as family. One day, he would tell them how much they had meant to him and his mom.

* * *

Sam Justus was a sixteen-year-old, blond-haired, blue-eyed demon. They all called him that behind his back. He was a recovering addict and was having a tough time with it. Starting fights, stealing, acting out. The crew were optimistic, though. His one redeeming quality, besides being good looking, was that he could cook better than anybody. That's why they kept him around. The staff, as well as the boys, would brag about his cooking. That pleased Sam. He had enrolled in a couple of classes that a local chef offered in German cuisine. One day, Sam wanted to open his own restaurant. That had always been his dream.

Sam's parents had left him and his two brothers. They had overdosed on prescribed opioids. For three years, Sam kept them together by working in a local restaurant, cleaning, washing dishes, and taking out the garbage. The owner had taught him how to cook and let Sam take home everything he needed. He knew the situation and had given extra money to Sam. One night, the man had heart attack, and everything fell apart. Sam and his brothers were separated. Sam got hooked on drugs at his first foster house.

He vowed that, one day, he would reunite with his brothers. Rick Morgan promised Sam that he was working on that situation. For the first time, Sam felt hope. It had been thirteen months.

* * *

Jasiel Flores was a 15-year-old boy who had come across the border with no name and no papers. He spoke little English and was studying hard. He had been working with a group of Mexican illegals that earned a living harvesting fruit. Some goody goody social worker thought placing him in the system was better for Jasiel than the situation he was in. He had been with a nice family and was saving all his money. One day, Jasiel was going to buy a house and hire a detective to find his real family for him. He needed to know why he was missing memories of his past. He must have a family—people that were looking for him.

* * *

Last, but not least in the slightest, was Antoine Miller. A 16-year-old sweetheart. He was a chubby little guy who everyone loved. He had the best personality—funny, joking all the time. Antoine loved Sam. No one knew why, and Sam was good to him. Antoine was the only one Sam would tolerate.

Antoine loved the movies and dreamed of being the next Denzel Washington. His father was in jail for shooting his mother. Antoine did not talk about them or his past. He was doing well in school now, and his grades were excellent. A very smart, little guy. His favorite chore was helping in the kitchen. He loved doing the dishes. No one knew why and no one cared because that was their least favorite chore. He had always helped his mother and grandmother with cleaning up after meals. He could hear the laughter. Bill Withers in the background.

Overall, the house was peaceful, and the boys were progressing right long. Everyone was thrilled at how well it was going with the first group.

Rick and Jesse

Rick was not impressed. Rick and Jess had met up with Dan Jenkins at an IHOP near Dan's business. Yesterday afternoon, the paternity test had been verified, so the meeting was a go.

It was not much of a business—a junk yard, maybe, that no one had purchased from in over ten years. The business card was misleading. It implied that there was an actual money-making attempt happening.

"I can't get over how much you look like your mother," Dan said to Jess in between gulps of coffee and mouthfuls of pancakes.

Dan had been doing most of the talking. Jess carried a photo of him and his mother in his wallet that someone had taken of them at Christmastime, and yes, Dan was correct. They looked very much alike. His mother had been a beautiful woman. Dan had explained that he had been young and leaving Jess was a mistake.

"But I'm here now," Dan continued. "I want to make it up to you. What do you say, son? Want to give us a chance?"

Jess didn't know what to say; he hadn't spoken much in the last thirty minutes and had nodded occasionally.

"I do have some questions," Jess said. "I guess it would be okay if we were to meet again and hang out."

"You could come over to the house for dinner next week," Rick said, knowing that he had the week off.

It was July the Fourth. The company he worked for always closed down that week for truck repairs and updates. Rick used that week to work on his own truck and to get some things done around the house he usually didn't have time for. Jess had already volunteered to help. This way, Rick would be around. The house would be a good meeting place. Rick could keep a close watch. Rick didn't know for sure why yet, but he didn't trust Dan, and although Jess had been through a lot, he was a naive kid in many ways.

Breakfast ended with handshakes and an acceptance of the invitation to the Fourth of July celebration at the house. Everyone would be there—Hank, Katherine, Lori and Jeff, the boys from both homes, Rick's sons and some of the neighbors, and now Dan Jenkins.

Frank

D an wasn't the only one looking for Jess.

The law office of Frank Bennet in Harlan County, Kentucky was hard at it today. Frank was sitting behind his desk that was covered in over 100 items, which his 73-year-old secretary, Bonnie Matney, marked as urgent. Frank needed to look at those today.

Bonnie set Frank's black coffee on the corner of his desk and sauntered out quick and agile like she owned the joint and he worked for her. Frank laughed. Bonnie was feisty and worked harder than the rest of his staff of eight put together. He put his glasses on and picked up the first folder on the stack. Bonnie always put her favorites on the top, and that's the way Frank had worked it all these years. He wasn't about to change his ways now.

In the folder, there was a note on a yellow sheet of paper that had been folded over a couple of times. He recognized the handwriting of his old friend, who had recently passed away. The note read:

Frank, I need for you to find my grandson. He gets everything.

The note was signed "Jim Daton Robinette" and dated the day of his death.

Frank folded the note exactly the way in which he had found it and placed it in his desk drawer directly in front of him. He looked over at Sally, his English bulldog, that sat in the corner of his office on her monogrammed cushion.

Frank whistled. "Sally, we have work to do."

Dan

Dan Jenkins was sitting at his desk, drinking a beer, and thinking about the day's events. Spending time with his son and pretending to be interested was harder than Dan thought it would be.

But Jess seemed to buy his act, especially when Dan pulled out that photo of Jess and his mom. Dan had found it in an old toolbox and just left it there. That decision had paid off. He wasn't so sure about Rick Morgan, though. That man had a way of looking at Dan that made him uneasy, but Dan comforted himself with the knowledge that it would all be worth it in the end.

Rick Morgan would be out of his life, and if Dan played his cards right, it wouldn't be much longer. Jess was really falling for the whole, "I-loved-you-and-your-mother act." Dan was just *young and scared*. Which was true, but he had been with Beth for one reason, and when he saw that wasn't going to happen, well... he just left. No looking back.

That was until he picked up a newspaper at a diner that he had stopped in on his way back from a fishing trip. He had been drinking a cup of coffee and having a piece of peach cobbler that was advertised as the "best ever made." Well, it wasn't, but he was hungry, so he finished it off. An obituary caught his attention.

Dan pulled on his glasses after recognizing the picture of the old man. Dan couldn't believe it. 83-year-old Jim Robinette had passed away in his sleep on Tuesday, the obit read. Funeral services would be held the following Saturday. He was the last surviving member of his family. *Well, good,*

Dan thought. *The old man had died alone and hopefully miserable.*

Dan wiped his mouth with the back of his hand, paid for his breakfast, and headed out to his old Ford pick-up truck with a smile on his face and a new game plan.

Rick

Rick Morgan had been home for four days. Worked at least fourteen hours each of those days so far. He had a lot on his mind, and he thought better and worked things out better in his mind with a goal in his head and a tool in his hand.

He had a gut feeling that something wasn't right with Dan. He said all the right things. Rick knew that Jess was slowly warming up to Dan, because Dan knew how to say what Jess longed to hear. Especially stories about his mother, Beth. Jess was hungry for details about his mother's childhood, and his own. The pregnancy, the story of Jess being wanted by both parents.

Dan blamed his poor choices on his background. Being eighteen and scared. Scared of Jim Robinette, for one. He had an opportunity to work for his Uncle Sam, the business Dan now owned. Sam had left it to Dan; there had been no one else. Then, Dan heard that Beth had married, and he was happy for her and took the easy way out. But of course, his story was that Jess had stayed on his mind all these years, and one day he decided he just couldn't take it anymore. He reached out to Jess. It was the best decision that he had made in a long time.

Rick just hoped that all of this was true. In the meantime, he and Hank and Grace were keeping a close eye on the boy. Hank came over when he could when Rick was on the road. Rick didn't know what he would do without Hank. Hank took care of business, and he took care of the boys. It was comforting to Rick to have Hank around when he was on the road, as well as Grace.

In three days, they were going to have a big get-together for the Fourth. Rick and Hank were going to pick up some fireworks this morning. Probably take some of the boys, or all the boys, if they wanted to go. They would no doubt stop at the new Mexican restaurant out on 57. It had become the boys' favorite. Hank's, too. He was the one who had mentioned several times to Rick over the last two weeks that they should go again, and he was no doubt the one who had mentioned it to the boys.

The newest Marvel movie was coming out; that was on the list for tonight, too. Rick had better get a move on. He smiled thinking about the evening ahead. He turned up "Night Moves" by Bob Seger on Pandora and started turning some bolts.

Dan

Dan was actually working today, working on his old Ford. It would not start for him this morning, so here he was, doing something he wasn't good at. He may have to take it to Steve's Automotive down the street, or else call Bill to come over and tow it.

Dan had been thinking about his past with Beth. All of that talking about her had brought back memories. Dan had really liked Beth, but he hadn't loved her. He wanted the easy way out and the good life. Beth was that for him, but after Old Man Robinette showed up one night at his bedside with a .45 cocked and slammed hard in Dan's left temple, he knew to get up and get out right then. His best option was to do as he was told.

He could still hear the voice in his head: "Son, you will leave here one way or another tonight. It is your choice how you leave. You will stay away from my Beth. Take the money and leave. Not looking back appears to me to be your best option, but of course, it is up to you."

The gun barrel was shoved harder into the side of Dan's head. Dan did decide to take the bag of money Jim had thrown onto his chest. Dan always took the easy way out. Jim had watched him as he walked out the door in his boxers and nothing else.

Dan did stop long enough to pick up his boots by the door. The keys were always kept in the ignition switch of the truck. Turns out, Jim had given him $25,000. It didn't take Dan long to go through it. It was a good time while it lasted.

Dan felt pretty confident one night, so he drove back to the shack in the woods that he and his dad had called home. His dad had left one night over a year ago, never to return. Dan pulled up in his newly purchased, used truck to have a look around with intentions to move back in. But the house was gone—burned to the ground.

Dan promised himself that night, under a full moon and smoke-scented air, that if he ever got the opportunity, Jim Robinette would pay for what he'd done.

Lori

Lori had just gotten off the phone with Rick. He was worried about the Jess situation. She was too.

Lori was five months pregnant and working all the time, but she and Rick still talked every day. Sometimes it was just a text, but it was always some sort of communication. Rick was still driving, working with the boys, working on his truck. He was helping Hank and Katherine, too.

After the conversation with Rick was over, Lori sat at her desk a little longer, thinking about the Dan situation. Thinking about how she hated Dan Jenkins and everything about him. She found it hard to believe he was Jess's father. She hated the way he laughed, talked, walked, and even breathed. He gave her an uneasy feeling.

Rick had invited Dan to the celebration this coming weekend. She and her new husband, Jeff, were attending. She knew that Rick was keeping an eye on Dan, but she didn't like that he would be there. They were all hoping Dan would not show up. They all wanted the best for Jess, and he seemed happy that Dan was coming; that's all that mattered. She knew that Jess's well-being had been the driving force behind the invitation. Jess would have met with Dan one way or another, Rick had said, and he figured this was the best way.

Lori was in a good place right now, and she wasn't going to let thoughts of Dan Jenkins rob her of any of her joy today, so she put these thoughts away for now. She pushed away from her desk, stood up, and gathered her things. She had a home-cooked meal waiting for her at home. She patted her stomach, smiled, and headed out the door.

Leaving everything else for tomorrow.

Katherine

Katherine was worried about Hank. He had been so tired lately, but she could not get him to slow down. Two sets of boys and he was working all day, up until one or two in the morning most days. Doing repairs and having long talks with the boys. The boys were also helping with the repairs, which is why it took so long.

Katherine was also worried about Jess. She hated Dan Jenkins. She had never met him, but he had cast a cloud over a perfect day.

There was a lot of planning and energy going into making the perfect day for the boys. Everyone was so excited about their first Fourth of July celebration as a family. Both sets of boys got along so well. Hank had said that they now had enough boys to play a decent game of baseball—his favorite sport.

Hank and Rick were very close, and when Rick was worried about something, he turned to Hank for advice and vice versa. Hank had a military background, so from time to time, he could call on old friends to pull up information on people of interest. Nothing appeared on Dan Jenkins. Now, that was a shocker.

Everyone who had met him had nothing good to say. That says a lot about a man. Katherine would meet Dan on Saturday, so she would wait to form an opinion then, but for right now, she wasn't a fan. She didn't expect that opinion to change.

Katherine turned on the little TV she kept on the kitchen counter. The Five on Fox was on. She began making chili for Hank and the boys, as well as keeping herself informed of the daily events.

Hank

Hank was headed to Rick's. He and some of the boys were having a night out—dinner and a movie.

Hank could not believe his life right now. It was full and good. He owed it all to the Butterfly Man. Hank laughed. That seemed so long ago. A new wife, a new life, a new focus, and a bunch of boys to raise. Hank had never been happier.

Rick had saved Hank. Pulled him up, out of one life and into a better one. Rick had given him friendship and introduced him back to the world. A beautiful world. Hank felt so good about the work he was doing with Rick and Katherine. They were making a difference, setting the boys back on track. Giving them a life where possibilities were endless and you could set your own limits, where the past has no power over your desires. Where peace was achievable. He was getting philosophical in his old age.

After reaching the age of 66, Hank knew a few things, and he wanted to instill that knowledge into the boys now so that they could arrive at a good place sooner than Hank had. That way, all of life's lessons that Hank had learned would not be wasted and could help the boys achieve balance and peace earlier in life. Then, it would all be worth it. Every second.

Hank had been hard-headed. He had received some good advice but chose to ignore it and made his own way on his own terms.

"And that is how we all feel at eighteen, I guess, but I am still going to try," Hank said out loud. "Great, now I'm talking to myself."

Hank laughed. He turned the radio on in the truck and headed for Rick's.

Rick, Hank, and the Boys

Rick, Hank, and the boys had a blast. The movie was good, and the meal was better. They were headed home with enough fireworks to light up the neighborhood. Rick and Hank sat up front talking. Four boys had come with them—David, Antoine, William, and Sam, plus Matt. The boys had invited him along. Rick approved.

Everyone loved Matt. Scott, Steve, and John had met them at the movie and had followed them to the restaurant. They helped choose the fireworks, just like they had done as kids. The Fourth had always been a big holiday for the family. Rick grilled food, and Lisa had made side dishes and desserts that they all looked forward to. No one could touch her chili. Lisa enjoyed cooking for their boys.

Rick had tried to make her chili for the boys last week, but it wasn't the same. They still thought it was so good. She would be glad that he had tried, though. He could feel her presence, and it made him feel good that he could still make her laugh, even though it was only in his head.

Scott had called earlier. Kaylynn wanted to spend the night with Paw Paw Rick. So tomorrow night, Scott and Laine would drop her off after dinner. He could not wait. After the boys were delivered home safely, he would have to head out and do a little shopping. Pick up some snacks for Kaylynn. Lots of ice cream and popcorn.

Rick

"Hey there, Mr. Morgan."

Rick had turned the corner, heading for the check-out lane at Food City with fifteen minutes left before closing. He missed the days when the grocery store stayed open 24 hours a day. Because of his work hours, it was convenient to do the shopping late at night sometimes.

He looked up at the sound of his name being called to see Dan Jenkins standing in front of him with a 12-pack of beer in one hand and a loaf of bread in the other. What was he doing here this time of night? He lived quite a distance away. Dan answered the unasked question.

"Been doing some fishing," he said. "On my way home. I knew that I needed some bread, and I was thirsty too." Dan smiled, holding up the beer.

Rick said, "Will we be seeing you Saturday?"

"Wouldn't miss it," Dan said as he headed toward the check-out lane. "Hey, say hi to Jesse for me."

"I'll do it," Rick said.

Dan left the store. Rick paid for his groceries, loaded up the Dodge, and headed home. Rick didn't like running into Dan so near the house this late at night, but the fishing was good here. They were near the lake. Beautiful area, lots of camping and hiking this time of year. It was strange that Dan was this close and hadn't contacted Jess, though, or invited him to come along.

Rick put these thoughts of Dan aside for now, forming a to-do list for tomorrow in his head. The list would start with a trip to Harbor Freight for parts for the Kenworth. He needed to change oil and grease the truck. Jess would be helping with that. Rick looked forward to the morning. He applied a little more pressure to the gas pedal and headed home with both front windows down to allow the soft breeze and night sounds to mingle with the music from the radio playing softly in the background.

Dan

Dan had been fishing with some guys he had recently met. One of them, Ben Adams, had a really nice fishing boat for sale, and Dan said that he would like to buy it, so the guy offered to take him out fishing for the day to show him the boat.

Of course, Dan didn't have the money right now, but he had been living on the dream lately that his dry spell was about over. It never occurred to him to ask Jess to go with him. It had been bad luck running into Rick Morgan. It made him look bad, being this close to Jesse and not checking in to see if he might want to go. Dan would come up with some excuse if Jess mentioned it. Dan had a talent for that.

As Dan was getting closer to his home, he popped the top off his third beer. He had been drinking on and off all day with the boys, and there was no point in stopping now. Dan was actually a better driver drunk. It took a lot to get Dan drunk. Usually, a few beers wouldn't cause much damage to his driving skills.

The boys had also invited Dan to fish on the Fourth. He would much rather do that than go to Rick Morgan's for the day. The thought of playing the part of a good dad all day for Rick and Jess as well as a bunch of strangers wasn't something that Dan was looking forward to, but he would have to bite the bullet. Dan was determined to pull this off, and he didn't have another plan for his future right now.

Plus, the idea of sticking it to Jim Robinette brought him immense joy.

Lori

Jess had spent a couple of days with Lori and Jeff. He had helped paint the nursery as well as done some repairs in the house and two of the restaurants. He was working at one of Lori's restaurants when he was off from school or had a long weekend. Jess was a hard worker. Rick had taught him well.

Jeff had slowly gotten over how Jess and Lori met. They all laughed about it now. Lori knew that Jess must've felt awkward around her at first, and dirty looks from Jeff hadn't helped matters any, but eventually Jeff forgave the boy for his actions, and he and Jess were quite a team. They worked well together. Life was strange sometimes.

Lori always thought things happened for a reason, and she and Jess had met for a reason. That reason was a big change for her brother, Rick, and a new direction for his life as well as Hank's. Hank met his new wife because of Jess. So, even though Lori and Jess had a rocky beginning, it had turned out to be a great thing. God did work in mysterious ways. Her mom had said that so many times, and she had been right.

Lori stood in the center of the newly painted nursery, admiring the mint green and neutral colors with her hands on her hips.

"Hey, Jess, I've got a great idea for the bookshelves," she called out. She could hear Jess's footsteps bounding up the stairs.

Bonnie and Frank

Bonnie Matney was a force to be reckoned with. Everyone in town, and many surrounding towns, knew and respected her. She had worked with Frank since day one. Her sleuthing skills were famous. When she started on a case, nothing could get in her way. She was tenacious, strong, and smart.

Frank had given the missing grandson case to Bonnie. She had found him in 36 hours. She had also located Rick Morgan. Rick had a good, honest reputation. At least the boy had ended up in a good place. Bonnie was very pleased with all the information she had received on the boy's home, where Jesse now resided.

She had turned all the information over to Frank. Frank had called Rick, and now Bonnie and Frank were on their way to meet with Rick so he could explain the situation concerning Jess and his newfound wealth.

Dan

Dan had left Jesse a message yesterday to call him back when he could.

Dan formulated a good excuse for being in the neighborhood and not contacting Jess, just in case. It was unusual for the boy not to call right back. Dan was concerned but not enough to try again. Tomorrow was the big day. He would just show up, turn on the charm, and repair any damages caused—if any.

Matt

Matt was having a big day. He had taken William, David, Antoine, Sam, and Jasiel to a quick drive-thru lunch at Taco Bell.

He then dropped them off with Grace and the new team member, Teri. Matt usually took his lunch break at the house, but he needed time to himself today. He was heading to the local mall.

He had told his mother last night that he was going to ask Grace to marry him. Grace was the one.

He loved Grace's kids. He and Grace were doing great work together at the house as well. She was fantastic, beautiful, and smart. He couldn't imagine a better person to spend the rest of his life with, and who knew—maybe one day, there would be a child of their own.

His mom had approved. She was so ready for her 43-year-old son to be married and happy and to give her some grandchildren. She loved Grace. Her son had never been happier, so she was totally on board. He couldn't wait. He hoped Grace liked the ring he would pick out for her. His mom had offered to give him hers, but Matt wanted to do this on his own. He had respectfully turned down his grandmother's ring as well. Matt wanted to give Grace a ring of her own that no one had ever worn.

Matt stepped out of his Jeep and headed for the front entrance of the mall with pure joy in his heart mixed with excitement. He was practically skipping. He laughed to himself and headed for the jewelers.

Rick and Hank

Rick and Hank had worked all day. Mowing. Painting. Prettying up the place for tomorrow—a phrase Rick's mother used when she was getting the house ready for company. He and Hank had stopped to have lunch at a local place that served beans and cornbread, after a quick trip to Lowe's for some more nails and paint.

"How did your sleepover go?" asked Hank.

"Oh, great," Rick replied. "We had a blast. By the way, that reminds me. I need to do some cleanup inside the house before tomorrow, around the kitchen."

Rick laughed. He and Kaylynn had built a fort with every blanket, towel, sheet, and rug that Rick had on hand, plus a few of his jackets. They had placed them across the chairs, stools, buckets, and step ladders from outside. He had torn down a section or two of it as he came through the living area this morning to get to the coffee pot. He would work on it later. They had made ice cream sundaes. Remnants from that were still on the counter. Rick would clean that up, too, so they could do it again.

"So, is Dan still coming Saturday?" Hank asked.

"Looks like he is," Rick said. "I think it will be fine. We will all be there, laughing, having a good time. They'll be so many of us there that he won't even be noticed. Jess is excited about Dan coming. It will all work out."

"Yeah, well I hope you're right."

"Me too."

Rick paid for lunch, and they got back into the truck. Rick checked his phone as he was pulling out of the parking lot. He had three missed calls. He listened to the lengthy message and called the number given immediately.

When Rick got off the phone, Hank said, "What was that all about? From the look on your face, it wasn't good."

"That was a lawyer representing the estate of Jim Robinette," Rick frowned. "He says it concerns Jess. He wants to meet and discuss the situation in the morning. I said that I would be there. You wouldn't have time to go with me, would you?"

"I'll make time," Hank said.

Rick, Hank, Bonnie, and Frank

Bonnie and Frank agreed to meet at a local restaurant near Rick's. Rick thought the people sitting across from him couldn't be more different. The assistant, Bonnie, was a tiny little thing. Dressed like a protestor he had seen on TV from the sixties. Frank was clean-shaven and dressed in a dark blue suit with a matching tie. He had perfect posture and a short, neat haircut. Business all the way. Rick liked them both. They were different but equally professional.

Bonnie and Frank sat on one side of the table. Rick and Hank sat on the other. Everyone had ordered black coffee. Turns out, Jesse had a grandfather named Jim Robinette. Jim wanted everything to go to Jess, his only surviving relative. His grandson.

Bonnie had been doing most of the talking up to this point. Finding Jess was their main concern, as well as learning Dan's intentions. Turns out, Dan had been bragging to a fishing buddy that he was about to come into money. Looking to buy a new house, a new boat, which created some interest around the small town.

Bonnie had posed as a woman looking to buy a house near her grandchildren after retirement, so she was privy to the local gossip swirling around the realtor's office. She had rented a motel room near Dan's shop and followed him to the restaurant where they were seated today. Dan met his fishing group here from time to time. So, after eating here and getting friendly with the waitress that waited on Dan, Bonnie had acquired all the information that she would need. Bonnie was very good with people. She knew how to make people feel at ease with her, which led them to open up about others and their opinions. This was very valuable and could lead to the discovery you were seeking if you kept at it long enough. Bonnie was very patient. Her third husband taught her that. Actually, all four of her husbands had contributed to that.

Frank spoke, "We could talk to the boy when he's ready. I knew his grandfather very well. Jess may have questions for me. I know that this is a lot to take in. If there is anything Bonnie and I can do for you to make this easier for Jess, please don't hesitate to ask."

He handed his card across the table to Rick.

"Thank you," Rick said. "We will be in touch, I'm sure." Rick slid his wallet out of his back pocket and positioned the card in the front flap behind his driver's license.

"Bonnie and I thought it best to run this by you before we proceed," Frank went on. "The kid has been through a lot, and we wanted this news to be delivered as smoothly as possible. This will be life changing for Jess. It's a lot of information for a young man to deal with."

More details were discussed. The four stood up and said their goodbyes with assurances of follow-ups and a meeting to include Jesse next week. Rick paid for the coffee.

Hank had been quiet on the way home. He was giving Rick time to digest the situation he was now in the middle of. Jess had become a wealthy man overnight. Dan's interest in Jess after all these years was apparent. He had known all along.

Rick and Jesse

Rick was amazed at how well Jesse took the news. No one else at the house was to be told, per Jess's request. Jess wanted to think on how best to deal with this new information.

Frank and Bonnie had met with Jess on his own that morning, and Rick was letting them deal with everything. Jess knew that Rick was here for him if he needed anything. Hank as well. Rick and Hank were getting ready for the big day that would be happening in a few hours.

Jess made one last stop on his way home after his meeting with Frank and Bonnie, and that was to see Dan. This is why he went to see Frank and Bonnie on his own. Jess wanted Rick with him, but there had been something else he wanted to do today, and he thought it best if he did that alone.

Dan

Dan pulled into his driveway. He braked hard. He had brought a case of beer with him. Left two more in the floorboard for later. Dan had never been so angry. Dan sat down in the old rocker on the front porch, opened a beer, and drank two thirds of the can before taking a breath. He wiped his mouth with the back of his hand. Dan was not going to stand for this. This had been his only chance to turn this life of his around, and Rick Morgan wasn't going to ruin it for him.

Somehow, he knew that Rick was to blame. He had never liked Rick and knew that the feeling was mutual. Morgan had too much influence over Jess. Dan didn't like it.

He had woken up around nine this morning to a loud banging on the front door, which wasn't helping his hangover. He had flung it open to find Jess. Dan didn't ask him to come in. Jess didn't seem to want to, anyway. Jess explained the situation as he saw it. Didn't want to have anything to do with Dan. Called him a liar. Left crying, and his last words were, "I never want to see you again."

Dan never said a word. He slammed the door, grabbed his keys, and put on some pants.

"I need a drink," he said.

The Party

Katherine and Lori were helping Hank with the grill and serving food. Katherine took over for a while so that Hank could add some extra helpings.

"They're growing boys, Katie," Hank said. "They need more than that."

Sam walked away carrying a large dixie plate filled to the brim with food. One hand under the plate and the other with a large solo cup filled with fresh-brewed tea.

"Them boys need to be walking away with two hands under those plates," Hank said. "They can come back for the drinks. I want these to be two-handed plates, ladies."

Hank laughed. They all laughed as he took over serving the food. Then, Rick joined to help, and it was all over.

"With the two of them serving, we will be cooking again in an hour," Lori remarked. "Rick always likes too much food instead of not enough. He always sends home leftovers. There won't be any today."

Everyone laughed.

"I'll make another pot of chili," Katherine said as she hurried over to the house. "I have enough ingredients."

Scott, Laine, and the girls were checking on the flowers. When they pulled up, that is where Kaylynn went right away—to check on her butterfly family. There were a couple of butterflies hovering over her wildflowers today. Her favorites were the blue ones. They were a rarity. She squealed with delight every time she saw one. Baby Lisa mimicked her. Rick could hear them both from behind the house where he was.

Rick, John, and Sam were coaching the boys in a rowdy game of some kind of soccer.

Lori's husband, Jeff, was trying to go over the rules, but it appeared no one was listening. Jasiel and Antoine were arguing over the last goal. There wasn't one made. That was the argument. This was Rick's favorite kind of day. Sunny, breezy but not hot—the kind of warm that made you feel good inside. Alive and joyful. Rick excused himself from the game for a minute.

"I'm getting the horseshoes!" Rick shouted. He promised that they would play a game, and he'd forgotten to bring them out. He was headed for the storage part of the barn and ran into Jesse.

"Hey, son," Rick said.

"I've been wanting to talk to you," Jess said.

"Okay." Rick waited.

"I want to thank you for everything that you have done for me," Jess said. "I feel like for the first time in a long time, I belong. I have a home. I feel tied and anchored. It's a good feeling." Jess fought back tears.

"I love you, Rick," Jess said.

Rick hugged Jess, fighting back tears of his own. He said, "I love you, Jess."

Rick pulled free. "Come on, you can help me find my horseshoes."

He winked at Jess. Both men smiled and headed to the mess they called the storage building.

The Incident

It was around 11:30 p.m. The last of the fireworks had been set off. Most of the guests were heading out or gone. Lori and Jeff had stayed to help clean up with Grace. Rick and Hank were sitting on the tailgate of Hank's Toyota, talking and sipping the last of the sweet tea. Katherine was going to head out with the three boys from the home, and Hank was to follow with the other two shortly. The boys that were still at the house were watching the end of season one of *The Flash* or playing chess. Matt had been teaching them.

"Been a good day, hate to see it end," Hank said.

"Yeah, me too, but I have to get up early in the morning," Rick said. "Been a big week."

"Hey, at least we didn't have to see Dan," Hank laughed.

"Is that right?" replied Dan from the shadows. He was a little unsteady on his feet. Speech slurred a little too much.

"What are you doing here, Dan?" Rick asked.

"I was invited, remember?" Dan slurred. "Sorry I'm late."

Dan was leaning on the trunk of the old maple that grew along the fence line. Lisa had named it Jane, after a character she liked in a Thomas Perry novel. A series she had been reading right before she died.

"Dan, you need to go home," Rick said. "Hank and I will drive you."

Rick stood to Dan's left side, a few inches away. Both Rick and Hank had put down their glasses and were paying close attention to Dan. Then it happened.

Dan pulled out his revolver. Three shots made contact. Both men were on the ground.

Part Three

July 10

Scott

It was a beautiful summer afternoon. *Dad would have loved it*, Scott thought.

Puffy white clouds hung low and moved westward against a startling blue sky. Perfect for a family get-together. Instead, here Scott sat, waiting on the preacher to start the service.

Katherine was sitting up front, head lowered, and crying softly. The chair beside her was empty, waiting. Lori was on Katherine's left, holding her hand. The boys from both homes were sitting together. Some of them had elected to be pallbearers. They wanted to pay respect to the man who had impacted their lives so much. This man had no hidden agenda. He was simply trying to help lost boys find their way by giving them encouragement and advice. He had given the most valuable commodity a human being had to share—his time. He had a short time with them, and he'd made the most of every minute of the day. He had talked with them, worked with them, cooked, and built things with them.

Scott looked around at all the people sitting in the folding chairs, here to honor and say goodbye to a good man, knowing that they were all thinking about the impact this man had made on their lives.

Scott was remembering the last time they had all been together. They'd met up at Hank's favorite restaurant, and then went to see a movie. They selected fireworks for the big Fourth of July celebration, not knowing that they'd be rocked to the core a few hours later. This did not make sense to

Scott. He couldn't think right now. He had to be strong like his dad. Scott moved toward his wife and daughters to take a seat.

July 5

Dan

Dan Jenkins was lying on his back, looking up at the ceiling of the cell he had spent the night in, waiting on his lawyer. He had been arrested, but he was going to get out of this mess, just like all the other times. He would plead temporary insanity like most did, or something like that.

He had been so drunk; he really didn't remember driving over to Rick Morgan's place. He didn't have a memory of what he had done. He was drinking all day. The hatred had built up so bad in his chest, he could feel it. It was like someone tried to push a rock out through the front of him. He remembered looking for the keys. He had run out of beer. He got to the store, forgot his wallet. He had to go back. Then, he somehow changed directions and ended up at Rick's.

Yeah, thought Dan, *I'll work on my story, let my lawyer do the rest. That's a lawyer's job, right? Sell a story well told.*

July 5

Lori

The nurse had just left the room. Hank had gone to get some coffee. Rick was lying in the hospital bed, looking pale and gray. No color in his lips. IVs and cords were running from everywhere. Rick was in a coma, and for now the doctor could not give a lot of details. He had been shot two times. He had come out of surgery and was stable for now. Lori sat by Rick's bedside for hours, holding his hand, tears in her eyes. She had been talking to him mostly about when they were kids. Updating him about Hank's condition.

Hank suffered a flesh wound that had been treated. His shoulder had been giving him some trouble, but he was fine.

"I can't lose you, Rick," Lori said. "You're everything to me. I can't remember a time when you weren't there. You've been with me my whole life. You're my father, my brother, my friend. Please, God, don't take him from me. Not now."

She patted her stomach and squeezed Ride's hand harder.

"You haven't tried your hand at being an uncle yet, big brother," Lori continued. "Please open your eyes for me. I love you."

She stood and bent to kiss his forehead, just as he had always done when they were kids.

The first time Rick kissed Lori on the top of her head was when he had left to go to the Army, after they formulated the plan for her to live with their aunt. He had been quite a bit taller. Her heart broke at the sight of him walking away. Just like now. Lori stared into Rick's face, praying for a miracle with low expectations.

July 5

Rick

R ick was dreaming.

Rick was at the movie theatre with Lisa. They loved the movies. He hadn't gone since she had died except for the other night with the boys. They had been so excited and had wanted him to go. He and Lisa had gone to the movies at least once a week when they first started dating, and all through their marriage when they could. Then, with the boys—a different kind of movie, but they had loved it just the same.

Rick proposed to Lisa at a movie theatre. She had seen the proposal on the screen. He'd called the manager, and he put Rick in touch with some guy in New York that had put together a photo of him and Lisa with the caption, *will you marry me?*

Lisa thought they were on a date, just like all the other times, eating popcorn and waiting for the movie to start. She saw their photo on the screen. The look on her face and her squeal was worth it. She jumped up, forgotten popcorn flying everywhere. Rick had loved surprising her and making her happy.

"Lisa?" Rick said.

July 6

Hank

Hank hated the smells and sounds of a hospital. He especially hated being in one with his best friend. Rick was still in a coma. He had taken a pretty hard hit to the head. When he had fallen after being shot, his head made contact with a protruding stump. Hank tried to shield him. He had taken a hit and had fallen on Rick, which only added pressure to the impact. Rick had taken two shots—one to the arm and one to his upper chest. The head trauma was what the doctor was most concerned with.

Katherine had just left. She knew better than to ask Hank to come home and get some rest. She had brought a few things from home that he might need for the evening. Hank would sleep in the chair again, just like he had done last night. He would not leave his friend. April Brown, the day-shift nurse, had taken Hank to a room down the hall where he could shower. They were still monitoring him as well. The coffee was good, and that's all that he needed.

Hank was sitting in a chair by Rick's bed, thinking about the day they'd met for the first time. Rick had offered him friendship—something Hank didn't realize he needed. He owed Rick so much. He bowed his head to pray.

July 6

Rick

Strawberry Plains, Tennessee.

Rick had broken down there once. Lisa had to come and pick him up while his truck was being hauled back home to Sam Snead's garage. They turned it into a road trip. Lisa brought the Dodge instead of her Volvo so that they could stop at a nursery and pick up some trees for the backyard.

Rick mentioned passing the nursery. They had said that, one Saturday, they would go down and check it out. Peach, pear, and a few apple trees had been purchased and loaded up that day. They were to be planted on the lot by the barn. They stopped at a nice restaurant on the way home. Steak and crab cakes. Lisa's favorite fancy meal. The boys were still young, so pizza, nuggets, and fries were the go-to at home. You couldn't beat a McDonald's happy meal after ball practice. It just hit the spot. Ice cream cones and the best sweet tea money could buy in the drive-thru, at least three nights a week.

Then, as the boys got older, they moved up from the happy meals and ordered the grown-up versions. All through high school, no matter what town you were in, you could always count on the food being good and tasting the way you liked it and expected. Rick missed those days with Lisa and the boys. Everyone was healthy and happy, living their best life.

July 7

Hank

Scott, John, and Steve had just left.

Scott's oldest sent butterfly pictures that she had colored for Paw Paw Rick to hang in his room, so that when he woke up the pictures would be the first thing he saw. Scott brought the scotch tape Kaylynn had handed him to make sure her instructions would be carried out. Scott taped them on the wall in front of his dad. All fourteen of them. So, of course, a couple of the nurses were calling Rick the "Butterfly Man" after Hank explained.

Hank encouraged it. It would've made Rick laugh.

July 7

Jesse

J esse was fighting mixed emotions. He wanted to see Rick, but he didn't feel worthy. After all, this was his fault. Dan Jenkins was his fault.

Jess's biological father had shot the man that he considered his real father. Rick had been in a coma for three days now. Hank was shot while trying to prevent Rick from being killed. A flesh wound, thank God, was all it had been. Jess wanted to see Rick to possibly say goodbye to the man he loved.

He had caused this family so much pain. He had been forgiven, but he couldn't forgive himself.

Jess was sitting behind the wheel of a Dodge Charger that Rick had helped him rebuild. He was thinking of the good times they had working on the car together. Drinking Diet Pepsi by the case, eating Grace's homemade brownies. Grace would send over leftovers from dinner at the house from time to time, always bringing ice for the Pepsis. Sometimes, they put in a sixteen-hour day. These were Jess's favorite times spent with Rick. Rick was on the road a lot, and Jess was a full-time student, so time was hard to come by, but they had at least put in two sixteen-hour days a month no matter what was going on.

Jess was crying, head on the steering wheel, debating whether to get out of the car and walk to the front entrance of the hospital. Jess wiped his eyes, got out of the car, and walked with purposeful steps toward the double doors, knowing that he would be welcome and forgiven without asking. He wished he could forgive himself.

"Please, God, let him be all right," Jess murmured.

July 7

Grace

Grace was sitting by Rick Morgan's hospital bed, thinking of all the years she had known him. What a good friend he had been to her and the kids. She respected him above all others.

Grace was dating a good man right now. The kids had really taken to him, and that was the most important thing. She owed meeting him to Rick Morgan. Rick had given her a job at the boys' home, and that's where she and Matt had met. She liked him right off. He was so good to the kids.

Grace was crying but trying not to. Hank was in the cafeteria. He hadn't left Rick's side since the shooting despite being shot himself. He said he was fine and brushed off attempts made by everyone for him to take a break.

Katherine stopped trying to convince her husband to come home. She came by every day with a change of clothes and to bring him something to eat or to eat with him in the cafeteria. Wednesday was meatloaf and mashed potatoes day, and it wasn't half bad. It was good, actually. Katherine said hers was much better, but she followed Hank dutifully to the cafeteria.

Grace was trying to keep up the boys' spirits. They were so worried. She tried to hide her concern from them, but right here, right now, she was truly worried about her dear friend.

"Rick, please come home to us," Grace pleaded, squeezing his hand. "The boys miss you. Things just aren't the same without you. You must come out of this."

She was startled by the return of Hank and Katherine. Hank patted her on the back.

"He's going to be all right, Grace," Hank said with conviction. "He will come out of this."

Grace wanted to believe him. She stood up and retrieved her purse from the back of the chair where she had placed it earlier. A red one. Rick had given it to her for Christmas last year. She had mentioned to him once that she was looking for a red one when she left early one afternoon to go Christmas shopping.

Rick had said, "Well, maybe you should hold off on that purchase. You never know, you may get one from Santa."

She knew then what would be under her tree Christmas morning. They had decided to draw names at the house for Christmas. Of course, everyone bought for the boys, but the employees thought it would be nice to exchange and draw names. Grace figured Rick must have drawn her name out of the hat.

Now, Grace hugged Katherine and Hank goodbye.

"Please call if there are any changes," Grace said.

"Of course," Katherine and Hank both said. Grace walked toward the elevator, pushed the button for the ground floor, and cried all the way to the parking garage.

July 7

Dreaming of Lisa

Rick

Rick was working on the truck. It was early Saturday morning. The sun was warm on his back. He could feel the heat on his legs. They were protruding from under the hood of the Dodge. He loved working on his truck. He loved the feel of the metals in his hand. The smell of the oil. Getting the job done. It was satisfying.

He'd be heading out in the Kenworth soon. He still had to mow. Lisa would be making his favorite snacks for the road. Peanut butter no bakes were his favorites. They both hated the long weeks. This one coming up would make about twelve days out.

They had a ritual: Lisa would follow him out, waving and smiling until she couldn't see him anymore. Rick always tipped his hat to her when he first started out for good luck and a safe return. He kept his left hand out the left window, waving back until he couldn't see her anymore in the side window. She would blow kisses and smile until the taillights were no longer visible. He could see her so clearly in his mind. He could see that beautiful smile so clearly. She always made it so hard to leave, which he had told her several times.

"That's why I do it," Lisa said.

Rick's mind was growing cloudy. He couldn't focus. He took a last look and kept waving, smiling at the sight of her.

"I love you, too," he said.

July 7

Rick

"It's starting to look like Logan's in here," Lisa had said, laughing, referring to a local restaurant where the customers could throw peanut shells on the floor if they wanted, as she continued to get Betsy Blue ready for the week.

Betsy Blue was the name she and Rick had picked out for the Kenworth when they had purchased it. Lisa insisted on organizing the sleeper, making the bed, and stocking the cabinet with healthy snacks like Doritos, Slim Jims, and Oreos. Lately, Rick had developed a habit of eating peanuts in the shell. Their neighbor, Ron, grew his own and had given Rick a bag one evening. From then on, Rick was hooked. He had a bowl of peanuts in the floorboard and a Walmart bag to put the shells in alongside of the bowl. Sometimes, he would miss his mark. He liked a clean cab. Anytime he stopped for fuel, he would take the small straw broom out from behind the driver's seat and clean the floor. His dad had been neat and tidy from what Rick remembered, and of course it had been reinforced in the Army.

Clean barracks was a must. Lisa had said early on in the relationship that Rick's neatness was her favorite part of him. She always winked at him after making that statement. As she was folding the black tees and placing them in the shelf, she looked up and smiled.

"Do you want to maybe try another color?" she asked.

"No, I'll stick with the basics," Rick said. He grabbed her chin and kissed her forehead. "No need to try something new now. Black works out just fine in my line of work. I'd just ruin a lighter color, and then the shirt would be ruined and end up as a grease rag. You wouldn't want that."

"I love you," Lisa said.

"I love you too, babe," said Rick.

"It's time, isn't it?" Lisa said with sadness in her voice.

"I don't want to go," Rick said. Leaving for the week was a sad day, even after all these years. Lisa was trying not to cry.

"I will miss you," Lisa said.

"I'll be home before you know it," Rick said. He hugged her long and tight. She felt good in his arms. Her soft brown hair was blowing in the wind and tickled his nose. Rick could smell the sweet scent of her perfume.

July 5

Frank and Bonnie

Frank Bennet and Bonnie Matney were standing in the hospital room next to Rick Morgan's bed and directly in front of the window. The rain was coming down heavy. The region was under a flash flood warning. The rain was beating loudly against the window. That and the monitors were the only sounds.

Jesse had been sitting on the chair on the other side of the bed when they walked in. He looked up, acknowledging their presence with a nod and looked back down at Rick.

Frank knew from the few times he had met with Jess over his financial affairs how much Rick meant to him. How much Rick's entire family meant to Jess. He had explained to Frank and Bonnie over sandwiches and coffee in the office how they'd met. It had been a remarkable story.

Frank and Bonnie enjoyed working with Jess and helping him through the difficult transition of coming to terms with the death of his grandfather that he would never meet, and the effect the inheritance would have on his future. He was a good kid. He was going to be okay. Frank hoped that Rick would be as well.

Bonnie thought Rick was a very good-looking man. She had mentioned that opinion several times over the last couple of days. Rick had come into their office on his own. He wanted advice on setting up accounts for the boys, including Jess. It wasn't much, but in the years to come, they would have a little something to help them out. That wasn't Frank's expertise, but he and Bonnie had given Rick good advice and had helped with setting up accounts at Rick's local credit union. When Bonnie heard of the shooting on her broadband radio that she kept in her dining room, she called Frank immediately. She told him to get dressed and that she would meet him in fifteen minutes.

Now, here they were. Frank wasn't a bit surprised when Bonnie showed up in her pajamas, covered by a tasteful and very expensive raincoat. She hadn't wasted any time.

Rick looked pretty rough right now.

"What do you think, Bonnie?" Frank asked softly.

"I think that man is going to need a lot of prayer," Bonnie replied.

July 7

Amanda

Amanda Sargent was the nurse on call when they brought Rick Morgan into the ER, and she had kept up with his progress over the last three days.

His friend, Hank, had been by his side the entire time. He only left when someone could be with him, and that was only to get a quick shower or have something to eat. Never more than thirty minutes at a time. Just enough time to give the visitors enough alone time to say what they needed to say.

Amanda was worried about Hank. He did let her check on his wound without complaining too much. It seemed to be healing fine. He was in his late sixties. No sleep except what he was getting in the chair. He left to eat once a day, and that was probably because his wife came to remind him that he needed to. Katherine was a sweet lady. She had spoken to Amanda several times.

Amanda brought Hank some beans and cornbread and a piece of pie that her mother had made that evening. She noticed that it was all gone when she stopped by to check on her patient. Hank had been dozing in the hard, faux leather, green chair when she walked in. It was now ten o'clock at night. The hospital was quiet on the third floor.

Rick's vitals were good. Amanda knew the doctor was worried about his coma. It had been three days with no change. Amanda hung the fresh IV bag and turned to find a young boy sitting by the bed. He had slipped in quietly. Hank must've just stepped out.

Amanda hadn't met this young man before, but she was pretty sure he had been the kid who was here the night they brought Rick in. Visiting hours were over. Amanda could tell by the worried look in the kid's eye and by the way he was clutching Rick's hand that he cared very deeply for him. He was crying. Amanda would wait until Hank returned; she had some stats to record, and she would take her time.

The boy was whispering. She couldn't make out what he was saying, and she wasn't trying to. She was here if needed, doing her job. Being around when people were saying their goodbyes and resolving issues that should have been taken care of long ago was part of the job. People often realized that they wasted valuable time with their loved ones. Sometimes, people would confide in Amanda. She would talk and console them when needed.

"How is our patient?" asked Dr. Mitchell. The doctor had come in quietly.

Amanda looked up with her clipboard in hand to address the doctor's questions with the latest information.

July 8

Hank

Hank was dosing in the chair. His watch read *12:45 a.m.* He was thinking about a conversation he had the other day with one of Rick's boys about a man's past. It didn't define you. You shouldn't let it. Just because you are *this* today does not mean you can't be *that* tomorrow. A person changes.

"Look at me, for example," Hank said. "I was in the Army, got out, got married, and ran a successful restaurant. Life threw me a stumbling block, but I rebounded with the help of a good man. Now I'm living my best life. Doing something that I love and enjoy. Met the love of my life. I have some new friends, and a new family. A family isn't always the people you are related to by blood. They can be the folks you choose to make your family and the people that choose you. These are sometimes better."

He had laughed before continuing, "I'll have to tell you stories about my Uncle Joe. Nobody with good sense or in their right mind would ever choose good ole Joe for a family member or a neighbor, or anything on purpose. He sure was ornery."

Hank had stood up from the step he was sitting on.

"Let's run on in the house and get some supper," Hank winked at Sam. "I think we're having pizza."

The two of them passed the delivery boy coming down the steps of the front porch as they were going up. Hank opened the door to the front door for Sam to step through. He could taste the pepperoni.

July 8

Hank and Tommy Miller

M att wasn't the only one with an errand to run. So did Hank.
Lori was with Rick. She would stay a few hours. Hank knew that
Katherine would arrive by lunch time to check on him and Rick. Hank
had slept fitfully, to say the least, last night.

It was July 8, and Rick was showing no signs of returning to this world
today. Hank had not left the hospital this entire time. He wanted to be
there when Rick woke up from the coma. However, during the night, he
thought mostly of Dan Jenkins and how he had single-handedly ruined
every good thing that he and Rick worked so hard on that year.

Rick and Hank had opened up a home in which good boys could get
back on track. Rick and Hank had begun the process of healing from
wounds that life had inflicted upon them. Life was good again, and then
Dan Jenkins came uninvited into their lives. Now, Rick was in danger
of losing his life, and Hank was in danger of losing his best friend. Lori
and Jess were devastated. Rick's death would destroy so many lives and so
much good that had only just begun.

Hank showered quickly in a hospital bathroom that he was allowed to
use during Rick's stay. He called a friend to give him a ride to the jailhouse downtown. He told Lori he would be back shortly and met with
Tommy Miller at the front entrance to the hospital.

"Good morning, Hank," Tommy said as Hank settled into the passenger seat of his forerunner. Hank closed the door and put on his seatbelt.

Tommy hit the gas and headed toward their destination.

"Thanks for picking me up, Tommy," Hank said.

Hank had explained some of the situation to Tommy on the phone, so Tommy knew the plan. Tommy had served in the Army with Hank years ago. They kept in touch over the years. Tommy was a good man to have in a storm, as they say, and he and Hank had seen their fair share of storms. Tommy was dependable, loyal, and cool under pressure. He'd had an aneurism a few years back and lost some of his memory, but he was as tough as they come. Tommy was getting close to seventy years old and wasn't showing signs that he intended to slow down anytime soon.

"I'll wait for you right over there," Tommy said as he stopped in front of the jailhouse and pointed to the parking area to the left.

"I won't be long," Hank said. Tommy watched as his old friend walked towards the building, wondering if he should be concerned enough to follow him in or just wait as expected. He decided to stick with the plan and wait.

July 8

Dan

It had been a busy day for Dan. His son, Jesse, had paid him a visit basically to tell him off and to tell him that he hated him and would apparently forever.

Yeah, well, whatever, thought Dan. His lawyer had dropped by to talk about his defense. Two counts of attempted murder were pretty serious. Dan would plead temporary insanity for a reduced sentence, if it went that far. His blood alcohol level had been .07. That would not help his case, but his 28-year-old lawyer was bound and determined to get him a fair deal. Dan would be his fourth case and hopefully his first win.

Of course, Dan didn't know that, but he was sold on the confidence his lawyer was filled with. They were pleading not guilty, of course. Hank getting shot was an accident, and Rick wasn't dead. The intentions were not to kill him but to scare him. Hank and Rick had jumped at Dan and startled him, and the gun had gone off. It would really help his case if Rick survived. It wasn't looking good right now according to Chip Hurley, who told Dan this with a smile and a nod of encouragement. Dan's lawyer had been gone maybe fifteen minutes.

"You have another visitor," said a day-shift officer.

Dan couldn't imagine who it could be, and as the body emerged from the shadows, Dan saw it was the old man, Hank. The man who got in Dan's way.

"What are you doing here?" Dan asked Hank as the latter stood dead center in front of the cell with both of his hands gripping the bars, hatred in his eyes.

"I'm here to make you a promise," Hank said. "If they don't put you away, then I will."

Hank turned and walked out.

July 8

Jesse, Frank, and Bonnie

Jesse wished that he had gotten to know his grandfather. He would have liked to have formed his own opinion of the man, but that could never happen. Jess had been working with Frank and Bonnie on his inheritance and all that that entails, and of course Frank had been good friends with his grandfather over the years. Frank had met Jess's mother years ago.

Mostly, Frank and Jess's grandfather had played golf and talked business. Frank liked Jess's grandfather and spoke highly of him but couldn't explain the estrangement between him and Jess's mother. He could only council and advise his new client on how to invest his money wisely.

This was when Jesse missed Rick the most. Frank was doing his best, but he wasn't a substitute for Rick. Rick gave advice coming from a common sense approach to life. Jess missed working and talking with Rick. Those had the best times. He longed for that again. Sitting in the office with Frank and listening to his sound advice was not the same. Talking about wealth and the responsibilities attached made Jess feel restless and unsettled.

Bonnie came in with lunch from the White Birch across the street from Frank's office. They delivered and made the best chicken salad on toast, fried bologna, and grilled cheese sandwiches that Jess had ever had from a restaurant. Of course, you couldn't get any better than Grace's bologna and cheese on white bread with mustard, but Jess could appreciate this too, and he really did love Frank and Bonnie.

After they had fed the boy and Jess was on his way home, Frank and Bonnie started working on a few requests from Rick on behalf of a couple of the other boys at the home. Sam's grandfather was up for parole, and they'd found a lead on Antoine's uncle.

Since they had good news for the boys, Bonnie suggested that she and Frank take pizza to them after work. Frank agreed, and they both continued to work on some appeals for the rest of the afternoon.

Bob Waddell and Lori

Bob Waddell had stopped by the hospital to pay a visit to Rick while Hank was out. Lori was there when Bob entered the room. Bob did not know Rick well, but he was a fan. He explained to Lori how he knew of Rick after he introduced himself.

Bob was a truck driver. He was married with three beautiful daughters. He had been in a bad accident, and that had put him out of work for over six months while he was recuperating. He had fallen asleep behind the wheel. Rick had called a bunch of his friends that were also truck drivers after he heard the story, and they all adopted Bob and his family. They bought groceries, paid his utilities, and helped with hospital bills till Bob got back on his feet. The 20 percent was hard to come by with no income coming in.

Bob's family had been living paycheck to paycheck like most. He had never met Rick or any of Rick's friends, but they had been angels to him and his family during tough times. Bob heard about the shooting, and he wanted and needed to thank Rick for everything he had done, even if Rick wasn't aware. Bob wanted to at least show some appreciation by offering condolences to the family, if that were the case. He removed his hat and prayed for Rick before he left the room.

Lori was sitting alone after Bob left, thinking about how proud she was of her brother. Rick had never mentioned helping Bob. He had talked about Bob's accident, because it happened close to his route.

Lori had called him in a panic to make sure that it wasn't Rick who got injured. She remembered feeling so relieved when he answered the phone. She had sobbed with relief. He wouldn't have mentioned it to her otherwise, because he knew "accident stories" made her worry about him even more, so he kept tragic road stories to himself.

Lori was startled by a flutter under her hand that was resting on top of Rick's. She stared intently at Rick's face with hope in her heart. She put a hand on her stomach.

She was feeling a flutter there too, and then a sharp pain.

Bonnie and Frank

B onnie and Frank became regulars at the house over the past four days. They'd stopped by, at first, out of a sense of obligation to Rick. Frank and Bonnie wanted to help and offer their services of any kind to the boys and staff. They had fallen in love with the group and enjoyed spending time with the boys.

They had just finished playing a game of rummy, during which Frank had lost miserably to Bonne.

Bonnie was the one who suggested that they play, taught them all how to play, and ended up the big winner of the night. The big, old dining room table hadn't seen this kind of fun in a while. The table was littered with the remnants of the fun—pizza crusts, popcorn, skittles, and most of the cards. Bonnie helped clean up while Frank was led to the big screen for some Fortnite instructions. He was hooked.

"So, how was Rick today?" Bonnie asked Grace as the two of them sipped a cup of chai tea together at the kitchen counter, waiting on Frank and the boys.

"The same," replied Grace. "His color is better. Still no signs of coming out of the coma."

Bonnie patted Grace's hand and said, "It's going to be okay."

Grace smiled weakly at Bonnie, squeezing her hand in return and hoping against the odds that she was right.

"Excuse me," Grace said after hearing her phone ring.

July 8

The Nurse's Station

The Johnson County Medical Center's ER was busy tonight. There had been a fender bender, plus a heart attack scare. An older gentleman had been brought in by his wife with complaints of pain in his right knee and was unable to put pressure on his left leg after falling off a ladder. You could hear his wife fussing at him from behind the curtain, and that was the farthest room from the nurse's station.

Peggy Christian was putting some notes to Dr. Mitchell in the computer before she left for the day. It was midnight. She was tired. It had been a long day. Peggy had been there for over 17 years. She loved her job, and she loved the people she worked with. They were her family. She was the closest to Amanda. Amanda was like a daughter to her.

Peggy and her husband, Dennis, had raised three boys, who were all doing well in life. Amanda was the daughter she never had. Amanda worked the night shift tonight, so she was looking forward to talking with Peggy for a few minutes before she left.

"How's the Butterfly Man doing?" asked Jenny Campbell, a young lady who was a favorite of Peggy's. She had just received her RN degree nine months ago and was filled with energy and good will.

"He's had a good day," Peggy said. "No change. I checked on him about thirty minutes ago. I taped up one of his pictures that had fallen to the floor."

Rick Morgan was a favorite on the floor. This was his fourth day here. His granddaughter sent pictures of butterflies through her dad every day, and every now and again one would fall to the floor. Rick was a loved and respected man. He had many visitors—some who didn't know him well, a few who had never met him, but he had touched their lives in some way. They wanted to say thank you. Some stopped by to say a short prayer.

Rick wasn't expected to make it. He had suffered a brain injury, bullet wounds, and a blunt force trauma injury that was standing between him and living. Peggy kept telling the girls to expect a miracle; she had been witness to many over the years.

"Hey, Peggy, are you still here?" called Amanda as she came in with her pink scrubs and ponytail, complete with matching hairband and shoes, and of course a Tupperware container filled with treats for her co-workers.

She brought in something most nights, mostly homemade goodies, but sometimes something from the Walmart deli section across the road. It all tasted real good paired with a hot cup of coffee after everything calmed down.

Amanda had known Peggy all her life. She had dated Peggy's youngest son, Dean, in high school.

Peggy was the reason Amanda became a nurse. Peggy was the one who trained Amanda. She was Dr. Mitchell's go-to. Peggy knew everything about every patient. She was knowledgeable. She could have been a doctor herself, but she seemed content with her current title, which was "the boss." That was Dr. Mitchell's name for her. They were a great team, and Amanda was proud of the work they were doing here. It was a great hospital. For a small hospital, it had a great reputation, and Dr. Mitchell was highly respected.

Not only was Peggy a great nurse, but also she was a great babysitter. Amanda's only child, Liddy, had autism and Peggy was the only person Liddy would happily stay with. Amanda's first husband left her and Liddy when Liddy was just a baby.

Amanda had recently met a nice man named Chris. He and Liddy got along. Amanda was considering asking Peggy to babysit so that she and Chris could go out to dinner tomorrow night. She hadn't been out since the divorce two years ago. But before she could ask the question and tell Peggy the good news, the sound of a call button interrupted her thoughts.

The call button had been pressed in room 241—Rick Morgan's room.

July 8

Lori

Jesse had just left Rick's hospital room. Lori was still there telling Rick that the baby was kicking pretty hard today. Lori was waiting on Hank. He was in the hospital somewhere. It wasn't like him to stay away from Rick so long. Jeff was away on a business trip, looking at some cabinet doors for a customer. Lori had sent him to pick up a refrigerator part for the cooler at the main restaurant, so he would be home late.

Lori fell asleep and woke up with a crick in her neck and starving to death. She needed a snack. She would make a trip to the cafeteria when Hank returned. They served an amazing tomato casserole she and the baby would enjoy. She thought that she was having contractions earlier, but it was a false alarm. Maybe she should give Hank a call. She pulled her phone from the side pocket of her oversized bag.

"My suitcase isn't that big," Rick had joked one day. "What do you keep in there?"

"Only the necessities," Lori had said. "You never know what a day has in store for you, or what you might need. I would rather have more than not have something that I need. It's hard for me to live with regret. You know that. So, I prepare."

The call never went through. Jesse quietly walked through the door and gently tapped Lori's right shoulder. "How is he?" he asked.

Lori looked up, expecting to see Hank, but instead it was Jess.

"He's doing okay," Lori replied. "You know, talking my ear off."

Jess grinned. "He will again."

A sharp pain went through Lori's back and stomach. She grabbed Jess's hand. She handed him the phone that was still in her hand.

"Jesse," she started, "it's the baby. Call Jeff."

July 8

Jesse

Jess had been on his way to see Rick. He had figured out some things in his mind about his future and about the money. He knew exactly what he wanted to do after talking with Frank and Rick's son, John, who would be graduating from law school soon.

Jess wanted to talk it over with Rick, even though Rick would not be able to respond. He pulled into the parking lot when *bam!* Someone rear-ended his car.

Man, oh man. Jess jumped out to inspect the damage to his car and to blast the careless driver. The driver was the cute little blonde girl who worked at the local cinema. She was crying and apologizing as she got out of her car.

"I am so sorry!"

She looked up at Jess and stopped. It was dark and raining heavy. She went on to explain that she was here to see her grandfather. She got a call to meet her mom at the hospital. She had been worried and confused and didn't know if her grandfather was going to be okay.

"Hey, I know you," she said. "We have an English class together, don't we? I'm Kelli." She offered her hand for Jess to shake.

Jess shook her hand. She had soft, delicate hands and smelled nice.

"Yeah," he said.

He looked to the left at both vehicles. He checked the front of the little, red Volkswagen first. The damage was not so bad.

"Hey, I can fix the damage on both cars myself," Jess said. "That way we won't have to turn it in on our insurance."

The two exchanged numbers, and Kelli apologized again.

"I've got to go," she said. She ran towards the hospital, leaving Jess staring at her retreating figure, drenched from the rain. The damage to his precious car was forgotten.

July 8

Hank

H ank wasn't looking so good to his friend, Tommy, when he got back to the truck. He was pale and shaking. Despite protests from Hank, Tommy told the nurse on duty about their excursion when they arrived at the hospital.

Hank had been complaining of pain and soreness in his chest and arm. Hank gave him a sour look, but Tommy knew by the simple fact that Hank gave in to the suggestion of the nurse and followed her that his suspicions were right. Tommy thought that maybe Hank was suffering from a heart attack. That's why Tommy walked Hank into the hospital to ask for help.

They admitted Hank. Tommy called Katherine. She delivered some news to Tommy and made him promise not to mention anything to Hank about it right now. Tommy promised to stay with Hank until Katherine returned. It took over an hour for Katherine to arrive.

A flat-screen TV played on closed captioning on the wall in the small room. Hank was resting, his eyes closed. It had taken a while to run all the necessary tests. The three of them were now just waiting on the results. Katherine had been checking her phone constantly. All was quiet, with each person lost in their own thoughts. Then, a voice from the hallway broke the silence.

"Paging Dr. Mitchell. Room 241. Dr. Mitchell."

July 8

Rick

No one was in the room when Rick opened his eyes. Ironically, there had been someone with him around the clock waiting for the moment when he would open his eyes and come back home, and now that the moment was here, he was alone.

Directly in front of Rick was a self-portrait of Kaylynn with blue butterfly earrings on her elf ears. He recognized the drawing. She had made it for him during their last sleepover. Her crayons were still on the coffee table. She was wearing a crown. Several drawings covered the wall. Most were of butterflies or had butterflies in them.

Rick had been dreaming of Lisa—the first dinner in their new home, making plans for the future. Talking about painting their bedroom a shade of green. He was to make the final choice out of 100 samples Lisa laid out on the kitchen table.

"I will be happy with any of these, so you pick the one you like," she had said.

"They all look alike to me," Rick laughed. "I would rather you choose the color. That way, three years down the road from now when you want to change it, I can say, yeah, we should have gone with 32. That is the one I wanted."

They both had laughed then.

Lisa made spaghetti with homemade yeast rolls. It was her first try at sourdough bread, and it wasn't bad. She had worked with a starter for weeks. She had a mason jar on the counter with a weird-looking paste that Rick thought was glue. Now, that glue was covered in cinnamon butter, and it was so good.

Rick found a set of blue butterfly earrings for Lisa in a truck stop on his way home. He purchased them, wrapped, and presented them to her at dinner, and she immediately replaced the earrings she had on with her "new favorite pair."

Lisa said that about everything Rick bought her. She was easy to please and appreciated the thought more than anything else.

"The romance of it," she had explained. "You were thinking of me in that moment. These earrings represent the love you had in your heart for me." She pulled her hair to the side so Rick could see the earrings.

"Thank you," Lisa said. "What do you think?" She screwed in the second earring.

"Beautiful," Rick said.

"I love you," Lisa said.

"I love you, baby," Rick said.

Rick smiled. He could see the dining room table and the plant in the corner of the room that was twenty years old. Lisa's grandmother, Kate, had given her a start from one of hers. Rick saw the pineapple lamp with the yellow shade.

"Yellow is a happy color." No explanation was given for the pineapple other than that.

He missed Lisa so much. They had had such a good life. He wished it could have been longer. Then, thoughts began tumbling in from Saturday night. Hank, Jesse, Dan Jenkins.

Rick looked around and pressed the call button.

Part Four

July 10

Rick

Scott looked up from his phone, thanking God for his dad as he watched Rick walk towards him. Jesse had sent a message that he and Rick were on their way to the funeral earlier. Dr. Mitchell was not happy.

"Hey, son," Rick said. They hugged each other tight.

"Where did you get the suit?" Scott asked. "I didn't expect to see you here."

"A nice nurse named Peggy borrowed it from Dr. Mitchell for me," Rick said.

"You should have stayed at the hospital," Scott replied.

"I'm where I should be. Where are the girls?" Rick looked around. Before he got his answer, Hank had come up behind him.

"Hey, buddy!" Hank said. "It sure is good seeing you upright again." Hank was clearly fighting back emotion. He shook Rick's hand and squeezed his shoulder.

Rick smiled at his good friend.

"Thank you for everything, Hank," Rick said. "Jesse filled me in some on the way over."

"Looks like another hard day ahead for the boys," Hank said. "I hate that this happened to Matt. He was so good with the boys. He loved being with them. He worked over every shift. Bought things for them all the time. He taught them so much. One heck of a teacher. Grace is having a hard time, Katherine said."

Rick nodded gravely and looked over toward Katherine and Grace. He noticed Jesse sitting with a pretty young lady up ahead.

"Well, what have we got here?" Rick remarked. "I didn't know our Jesse had himself a girl."

"It just happened a couple of days ago," Hank said. "Love at first sight, from what I hear. Hey, we both know that happens."

"I'm happy for him," Rick said. "We'd better take a seat."

* * *

Rick sat in the back with Frank and Bonnie, who chose to maintain low profiles as well. Rick wanted to pay his respects to a man that had meant so much to so many. He had not wanted the focus to be on him. He didn't want to take away from the importance of saying goodbye to Matt. The man had dedicated his life to helping and teaching kids. He was an educator, a coach. He worked with the foster care program, as well as a local orphanage. He sponsored a sports program.

An aneurysm on the treadmill had ended Matt's life and had broken so many hearts.

Grace was sitting up front with Katherine. Hank was talking to Katherine quietly. Probably filling her in on Rick's arrival at the funeral. He nodded at Scott as Scott looked around to locate his father. Rick nodded, signifying that he was fine. Truthfully, he was feeling tired. It had taken a lot out of him to get dressed and walk the short distance from the car to the seat in the back.

The nurse had tried to talk him out of it but finally gave in after Rick explained the situation and promised to come back after the funeral. So, with the help of another nurse, they had borrowed some clothes from the doctor while he was on rounds and helped Rick to Jesse's car.

Rick would have the suit dry-cleaned and returned on his next visit. Hopefully, he would be officially released this afternoon.

Rick looked before him at the friends and relatives paying their last respects to a good man who was taken away unexpectedly. Rick didn't understand why he was spared, but he wasn't going to waste a minute of this gift of life. He made a promise to himself. He was determined to make the rest of his life stand for something good.

Rick was making a list as the Church of Christ sang "Wayfaring Pilgrim," Matt's favorite hymn, to honor their beloved member of over 20 years. Most of the congregation could remember the day of his baptism. What a celebration of life then and now.

To further pay their respects, the church had also given a sizable donation to Lisa's home for boys in lieu of flowers at Matt's mother's request.

Rick

Rick was officially released from the hospital two days later. Jesse had given him a ride back home so that he could take a shower and pick up his Dodge. Rick had some errands to run. After he dropped off Dr. Mitchell's suit at the dry cleaners, he went to see Dan Jenkins.

* * *

To say that Dan Jenkins was surprised to see Rick Morgan was an enormous understatement. When the guard came around to inform him that he had a visitor, Dan's last expectation would have been Rick Morgan. Dan was anxious, but he hid his emotions with his usual bravado.

"How's the old man?" Dan smirked. "He didn't look so good the last time I saw him."

Rick was not about to let Dan get under his skin. He recognized the statement for what it was. Dan wanted a reaction. Rick was here to disappoint. He chose to ignore the statement.

"If I thought you'd be a good father to Jesse, I would drop the charges and let it go, but we both know that Jesse means nothing to you," Rick said. "He's a good boy. A son to be proud of. He's had some difficulty in life, but it has made him what he is. He's going to be fine, and I feel like the best thing that I could do for him is to let you go to prison. That would keep you away from him for a long time, so that is what I am going to do. But Dan, I will pray for you. You had an opportunity to turn your life around and to be a good father. To have a family. I feel sorry for you."

"I don't want your pity," Dan said. "If I had known it was you coming to see me, I wouldn't have come out here. Get out!"

Dan got up. The guard came to escort him back to his cell.

Rick left. He climbed back into the truck, picked up his cell, and called Hank. They both had checkups at the hospital today. Rick and Hank agreed to meet around three o'clock. Rick would then go over to see the new baby at Lori's. Rick had some things he wanted to talk to Hank about first.

Rick and Hank

Rick had stayed for dinner at Lori's, and now he was heading back home. Lori was happier than Rick had ever seen her. She was so proud of the baby. Jeff was a good, supportive father. Lori seemed settled, and Rick couldn't be more pleased.

He was thinking back on the conversation he'd had with Dan. A pointless conversation. Rick needed to see Dan's reaction to what he said concerning Jesse. Rick hoped for a reaction of shame for what Dan had done. Remorse. Rick was hoping that after the alcohol wore off, Dan would be filled with regret and maybe have the desire to put things right with Jess. Maybe it wasn't just about the money.

But Rick sensed none of that in the man. He had meant what he had said to Dan. He would have dropped the charges and done everything in his power to help Dan renew his relationship with Jess if Dan asked for forgiveness and had remotely hinted at the possibility of starting over with his son. Rick guessed the hatred was real and fueled by the alcohol, not created by the alcohol.

People do things that they regret when they're drinking. Rick wanted to tell Jess that his father was sorry for what he did. Rick remembered how much it meant to Jess to have a chance to know his real father. That had been on Rick's mind this morning when he had paid a visit to Dan.

They would get through this situation together. Jess would heal in time and come to terms with the fact that some people will never change and nothing you can say or do will make a difference. Rick had talked with

Hank earlier, explaining why he went to talk to Dan.

Hank believed Dan belonged in jail. Jail was his destiny, and he deserved every year that he got. Rick almost died; Jess had been a victim of vengeance. Dan set out to get even and to take advantage, and Hank just couldn't get over that. He would help Jess in any way that he could. It was unfortunate, but it was something they would deal with one day at a time. They all had some healing to do. Physical as well as mental.

Time had a way of taking care of most things. Time and patience. They would eventually be able to move on. In the meantime, it was one step at a time. One step at a time.

*   *   *

Grace had given her notice at the house. She just couldn't be there right now with all the memories she had made with Matt. She was taking some time off. Taking the kids to the beach. Rick had given Grace an extra paycheck so that she and the kids could have a great time and do some extra things. She accepted the "bonus," as Rick called it. Matt's mother was going with them, too.

Rick hoped that the two women could help each other heal. They needed each other right now. They had become good friends.

Rick had two interviews scheduled in the morning at 9 a.m. and 10 a.m. Hank and Katherine would be there as well to help him through the interview process. It would be hard to replace Grace and Matt, but life had a way of moving forward regardless, and sometimes you just had to participate.

One Year Later

Frank Bennet brought in the last box from his black Volvo SUV. Boxes of files were scattered throughout the new offices of Bennet and Matney.

Frank and Bonnie relocated to Hartford, Kentucky after months of driving back and forth and spending time with the boys at Lisa's home for boys, helping with several situations. They were driving home late one night—a three-hour trip—when, out of the blue, Bonnie said, "Frank, I'm giving my notice. It's time to retire."

Frank couldn't believe what he was hearing. He knew how much Bonnie loved her job. She was the job. It was her life.

"Frank," she continued, "I have felt more alive and more needed than I have in years. I'd rather be here than anywhere. I've been thinking about it for a while now. I want to sell my house and buy one close to the boys. Something simple. I want to donate my time and my skills full time to the boys' program. They need me, and I need them. It's what I want to do. I hope you understand."

Bonnie knew that Frank would be upset. They had been together for 32 years. She had been dreading this talk for months now. She was surprised and a little hurt, truth be known, when Frank burst out laughing, pumping the steering wheel with the palm of both hands and shouting.

"Bonnie, you're kidding me!" he said. "I can't believe it. This is the best news. I've been thinking the same thing." Frank laughed again, louder this time. Bonnie couldn't believe it.

"We have been spending more time there than at the office," Frank continued. "I love driving down here for the day. I feel like I'm doing something wrong when I'm back at the office working on other cases. My mind has been drifting lately. How to help Grandpa get out of his drug charges. Getting Jesse through law school and all this mess with Dan Jenkins. I say we close up shop and move to Hartford. What do you say, partner? You and me, like always?"

"I say yes," Bonnie said. "I'll start packing tonight."

So, after completing a lot of the workload, promising clients that they would finish up cases from their new location, and hiring Samuel Reed to take over future cases that Frank and Bonnie would not have time for, they were all set. They also hired a receptionist, Debby Sargeant, to help Bonnie around the office mostly, and settled nicely into their new routine.

* * *

Bonnie took cooking lessons and was making dinner twice a week now. She got off to a rough start, but none of the boys complained, and when she got better at it after a while... well, no one complained about that either.

Of course, Sam volunteered to help, and the two of them became quite good chefs. Sam would eventually enroll in culinary school. Bonnie was so proud and took credit for giving him his passion for creating good food. He never told her any different.

Rick

Rick was heading home. He had just pulled out from the Pilot after filling up. $758.98. Everything was going up these days. The price of gas and groceries. It was getting harder to make a living for everyone. There was an oldies station on the XM. Sometimes good, old seventies rock and roll just soothed the spirit. Rick's spirit needed soothing after paying this gas bill.

Rick was three hours away from home. He would get home around 4 p.m. Hank and Jesse were working on Jess's cabin and had called Rick three times to add to his Lowe's list. Plus, he had a list of parts for the truck. He'd stop at Harbor Freight first. They closed early on Saturday.

* * *

Jesse had bought three acres of land beside Rick's property. It had a building, a little cabin, and a barn for a couple of horses. He wanted Rick to go look at a truck and a trailer tomorrow evening. Ron McClanahan, the old man who sold Jess the property, was also offering him a good deal on his fairly new Dodge with a trailer Jess would need for the horses he'd acquire.

It did sound like a great deal, but Jess wanted Rick's opinion. Rick felt like Ron would deal fairly with Jess without Rick's presence, but he agreed to go. Rick was proud of the decisions Jess was making with the money he had inherited. He was going to pay for school. Rick's son and Frank's influence had led Jess to go to law school. Jess was interning with Frank and Bonnie and spending a lot of time with Rick's youngest son.

Rick couldn't ask for a better neighbor. He had been surprised when Jess called with the news. Rick had known Ron was putting some land up for sale but never considered that Jess would be interested in purchasing it.

Rick and Jesse had worked on the blueprints themselves and found a couple of guys to help with the framework. The process was slow-going, but it was going well.

Katherine received a call from Grace yesterday. She was going back to school. She had always wanted to go into the medical field. She had decided to become a nurse. She was enrolled for the fall semester. Rick was so glad for Grace. She was a good person and deserved a good life.

Katherine had also mentioned that she and Hank had some exciting news to share and would tell Rick all about it when he came home. Rick had no idea what it could be, but he couldn't wait to hear. He was back on the interstate with good weather and good roads. He found himself singing along to "Tuesday Afternoon" by The Moody Blues.

Rick, Katherine, and Hank

After interviewing on and off for weeks, Rick, Hank, and Katherine decided on Teresa and Charlie Gentry. They were a retired couple who worked with AMIkids for over 30 years. Working with Foster kids had been their passion and life's work. Both were foster kids themselves, and when Teresa's mother passed away, she had wanted to be near her father, so she and Charlie moved back. When they heard of the job opening at the house, they jumped on it. They both really impressed Katherine and Hank. They were looking for a home and were trying to talk Teresa's dad into moving in with them.

After talking for several days, the four of them had come up with a plan. Teresa and Charlie would move into Katherine's home and run the boys' home from there, and Hank and Katherine would fill the positions of Grace and Matt. Rick couldn't have been more pleased. This would be perfect. The boys loved them already, so there were no transitions needed.

Katherine and Hank's boys were almost ready to leave, and Katherine was receiving applicants for new boys so that Teresa and Charlie would get an opportunity to form a bond with them right from the start, with no disruptions to an established routine.

Katherine and Hank had purchased a farmhouse two miles down the road from Rick's, and that was the big news. When they had time, they would start remodeling, but the first priority was Jess's cabin. They all agreed on that.

Rick and Hank

Another long day, but a very successful day. Hank, Jesse, and Rick were leaning against a newly placed fence they had built, admiring a job well done. They had just finished off a loaf of bread, a pack of thick-sliced bologna, and American cheese that Rick picked up at the Dollar Store, along with a family-size box of Nutty Bars.

"A working man's supper," Hank had said. "It doesn't get no better than this. You can put anything on a fresh slice of bread, and it will taste good when you're hungry. I may have said that a time or two before, but it's worth repeating!"

Hank laughed, finishing off his third sandwich. Jess had walked away from Rick and Hank to answer his cell phone.

"Guess that would be the girlfriend," said Hank.

"I guess so," Rick said.

"I think I will head on home and take a shower," Hank said. "I'll be glad when you go back to work so that I can take a break. I'm tired."

They both laughed.

Hank pushed himself away from the fence and continued, "Katherine is at the house helping Teresa out for a few days. I think she said they were getting new mattresses and painting at least two rooms this weekend, before the new boys arrive next week. Katherine really likes Teresa and Charlie. I think this new arrangement will work out just fine."

Hank wiped sweat from his brow. He never quit. He outworked them all every single day. He was the first to start and the last to quit.

"I think I'll do the same," Rick agreed. "A shower sounds good. I'm tired too. I think I'll call it a day. It's been a good one."

Rick followed Hank to his truck, rubbing his back and groaning a bit.

"You should come to church with me in the morning," Hank said. "Let me know, and I'll pick you up on my way through."

"Will do," Rick said.

"Be careful going home," Hank replied.

Rick nodded. He had no intentions of going to church in the morning with his friend. He smiled and waved to Hank as he pulled out. Rick had somewhere else he needed to be.

* * *

Every Sunday before he headed out for the week, Rick came to say good-bye to Lisa. He gave her reports on the kids. Brought her fresh flowers—usually white roses if he could find them. Sometimes he would surprise her. He'd see some pretty flowers that he thought she would like, and he would bring her those.

The boys came by on and off through the week and did the same. Rick would remove the dead flowers, brush off the marker, and clean up as best as he could, and add the fresh ones to the vase supplied by the cemetery. In the winter months, Rick used silk arrangements he had made at the florist that Lisa had used. Lisa's friend, Cindy Cordle, still owned the shop and always did a great job.

Sometimes, Rick would sit and lean against the tree across from Lisa. He enjoyed talking and sharing. He knew that she could hear him.

Rick had no way of knowing because his attention was focused on his storytelling and his time with Lisa, but Rick's weekly visits were talked about by the many visitors who also came by from time to time on holidays and birthdays to change out their loved ones' flowers. There were a few regulars like Rick. They could be heard saying phrases like, "He sure did love her," or, "I hate that that happened to him."

"There goes a man with a broken heart," one would say.

"Poor old Rick," said another.

"She was a good woman," remarked someone.

"She loved him too," someone agreed. "They were a good couple. They sure loved those three boys. She was beautiful inside and out. Wonder if he'll ever remarry?"

Rick's heart was broken, but he kept moving forward just the same. He was telling Lisa about the butterfly pictures that Kaylynn had sent him at the hospital. Rick had framed them and placed them on the mantle over the fireplace. All fourteen of them.

"That's what you would have done with them, babe," Rick said. His voice was breaking. He began to cry.

"I miss you so much," Rick said.

He sat there for a few minutes, emotion pouring through him. A butterfly landed briefly on his hand. He felt the soft wings touch before it flew away. The breeze catapulted the small creature forward, faster than it had intended.

That sometimes happens to people, Rick thought. *We are propelled in a direction by an unseen force that could have long-lasting effects.*

Rain was coming soon. Rick would've stayed longer, but he had to go to work. He was running late already.

"We always hated the leaving, didn't we, sweetheart?" Rick asked.

He stood, walked over to the marker, and pressed his fingertips to his bottom lip with his right hand. Then he pressed his fingers gently against her name on the marker. His pointer and middle finger, like always.

* * *

Hank was passing through town, and he saw Rick's truck getting on Exit 19, heading out for the week.

Hank's phone pinged. He picked it up from the passenger seat. It was a message from Rick.

See you next Sunday, it read. *11 o'clock for church. Maybe we can come back to the house after and make some chili for the boys.*

Hank smiled.

Epilogue

Lisa's home for boys continued and still remains standing and active in Hartford, Kentucky. Even during slow periods, the house remained open. Jesse Thomas saw to that. Having money that you didn't know what to do with came in handy.

Jesse became a good lawyer. He and John Morgan were quite a team. They took over for Frank and Bonnie when they retired. The law offices of Bennet, Matney, Morgan, and Thomas did a lot of pro bono work but were still very profitable, thanks to a few high-profile cases that always seemed to come their way.

Dan Jenkins served five years of his sentence and died from complications from a head injury received in the cafeteria. No one came to his funeral.

Hank lived to be 86 years old. He died peacefully in his sleep. He would have wanted it that way. His last day on this earth was spent working with Rick on a truck one of the boys had brought over.

Lori and Jeff ended up having three boys together. That house was chaos from morning until bedtime.

Grace became a registered nurse. All three of her kids received a college education. All three lived near their mother. She would become a grandmother to seven. Seven lucky children. Grace spoiled them all. She had remained close to Matt's mom over the years, and when Matt's mother died, she left Grace enough money to put a down payment on some land and an old house she had admired since she was a kid.

Rick Morgan never remarried. He did make peace with God and eventually taught an adult Sunday school class at his local church. He used his mother's old bible—the one she had written notes in the margin of. She had highlighted her favorite scriptures. Rick drew from these when he prepared a lesson. She would have loved that.

Hank kidded him one day, saying, "Well, you went from a Butterfly Man to a Preacher Man. That's quite a jump."

Rick had laughed. "I guess a man never knows God's plan for his life. It's never what you think it will be. If we knew, we'd probably mess it up."

Hank had nodded in agreement.

* * *

Rick continued driving through his seventies. He taught over 30 boys how to drive and helped them get their Commercial Driver License. They all drove for him starting out. He helped some of them get their first truck and to start their own business.

Rick had a good relationship with his bank manager; they went to church together. The First Bank and Trust had always supported the boys' home from the very start, and that help continued on as the boys graduated and moved along to becoming self-sufficient men. Morgan Transport developed quite a fleet. Quite a legacy.

Rick never missed a weekly visit with his wife. He was buried alongside her at the age of 84. His granddaughter, Kaylynn, had added an engravement:

Here lies my Butterfly Man.

The framed pictures above Rick's mantle were now hanging in Kaylynn's granddaughter's nursery.

* * *

Healing can manifest unexpectedly in many forms while the recipient is unaware. They may laugh again with no inner acknowledgement, unaware of falling back into old patterns, while the warmth of the sun soothes and calms the spirit. A person instantly responds to the touch of a breeze or admires the beauty of a monarch butterfly and are thankful without knowing that they were meant to observe and to appreciate the grace.

* * *

A scab sometimes leaves a scar, but the healing process happens just the same. A scar is a reminder of a change, a growth, or a renewal of spirit, and it can be beautiful. A scar is a reminder of the pain, yes, but also of hope and strength.

A lovely butterfly and a broken man had saved Rick Christian. Butterflies are tiny, insignificant creatures to some, unseen and unappreciated by many, but they have the power to comfort and to soothe—and isn't that what we should all strive to be?

Thank You

I hope you enjoyed my novel, *The Butterfly Man*. To all the readers who included this in your reading lists or recommended this to your book clubs, thank you.

If you find yourself with a few extra minutes to spare, I would love to receive your feedback in the form of a short book review. I encourage readers to post reviews on your favorite book vendor site or share a message with your friends through social media.

To keep up to date on my latest publications or to check out previous publications, visit www.jancarolpublishing.com.

To Mike Wade, it pays off to befriend a librarian.